Future's Past by David

# FUTUF

# By

# David j Henson

*Meet the Aothor your Sandhills Bar Man*

*Hope your loving it*

*D Henson*

# Future's Past by David j Henson

Future's Past

©David j Henson
The author asserts the moral right to be identified as the author of this work. All rights reserved. This book is protected under the copyright laws of the United Kingdom. Any reproduction or other unauthorised use of the material or artwork herein is prohibited without the express written permission of the holder of the rights.

All characters in this book are fictitious and any similarity to persons living or dead is entirely co-incidental.

First edition 2019.

Category: Science Fiction.

## FOREWARD

Over twenty years ago, I began an obsession that fuelled my imagination and a need to share that with others. I wrote a script that played with the idea of bringing an infamous killer back to life. I wrote the first draft but was never quite happy with it until my life was turned on its head and I found myself with a rage of emotion and no release for it. At this time, I didn't have a computer, but I realised that editing and rewriting the script in longhand helped me deal with what I was going through at the time.

I knew I had a story to tell and was determined to tell it. To date, I have had two attempts to get the script made into film, but finance was not forthcoming and thus my momentum stalled again.

Then I met someone who floated the idea of turning the script into a novel. I had thought of that before, but writing a book terrified me. After our talk I thought, why not? Thus, began the collaboration that not only moved the story forward at a record pace but added new directions and plot twists that I never believed possible. So here we are with my first book based on my twenty-year-old script 'FUTURE'S PAST'. I truly hope you enjoy reading it as much as I have enjoyed developing it.

There are a few people I must mention and thank unreservedly, and they are first and foremost, the author Nigel C. Williams, whose help and inspiration made this book a reality. Let me be clear, without his help this book would not exist.

To Nicole Faraday, Beric Livingstone, Russell Biles and Lizzie Goodridge, who saw potential in my story and helped cement how I saw the characters, I am grateful. And, to my family, friends, and to my beautiful children Emily and Ben, I know I haven't always been the best I could be, and I have made stupid and unforgivable mistakes, but you all stuck by me and believed in what I was trying to achieve. For that I want to thank you all from the bottom of my heart. This book is dedicated to you all.

THANK YOU,

David J. Henson

~~And to Monika my beautiful Peanut~~

~~Kocham Cię.~~

## PROLOGUE

**November 1982**

The darkened room was large and punctuated by a single circle of light from a ceiling mounted spotlight. A middle-aged man walked towards the light. He stopped in front of a glass case and peered at the item inside. The light above it was soft and designed not to cause any form of deterioration of the item. At nearly two-hundred-and-fifty years old, the shawl looked stained and distressed, like it had been dragged through mud.

The man pressed a combination of numbers into a keypad, he waited for the barely audible click that announced the release of the lock and removed the cover from the case. He gently lifted the shawl from the cushioned base and turned on his heel.

He exited the room into a brightly lit hallway. The walls were decorated with photographs of young, naked women, dozens of them. He paid no attention to the photographs as he walked along the hall of his forty-room Manhattan mansion.

A scantily clad young girl stood at the door to his bedroom. The man handed the shawl to her and watched as she placed it in an acid free bag before then wrapping it in tissue paper.

"Send it today. Get it to the airport and tell my pilot to guard it with his life. He's not to let it out of his sight until it gets to Heathrow. There'll be someone waiting there for it."

The young girl forced a smile and walked towards the stairs.

The man gazed at one of the explicit photographs and smiled. Smiling was something that didn't come easy to him. His face was usually impassive, his eyes constantly watching and absorbing the sights and sounds of the world around him, looking for opportunities to increase his enormous wealth and power within the higher echelons of society in America and further afield. He never understood why people trusted him, but they did. They seemed happy to tell him things that should never be divulged to anyone, things that should have remained buried. He had been the master tactician. The game was won. He smiled now because things were going to change. The personal fortune would finally be used to advance his goal, a goal that would change the world. No longer would he have to buy the favours of politicians and heads of state. Soon, they would be happy to openly declare their love and admiration for him. Soon they would all be seen for what they were – nothing more than animals with animalistic drives packaged within Saville Row suits.

### January 1988.

An arthritic finger rolled the focus wheel of the binoculars until the image of the running boy came into focus. The boy knocked the head off the snowman the other children had been building and was now silently laughing as he raced through the knee-deep snow towards a copse of tall, icing sugared pine trees at the end of the field. Just the slightest indication of a limp was present, it was something that no one would notice unless they knew the lad's history.

The sun flashed briefly through the grey shroud of cloud then hid once more as the binoculars panned from the running child towards the place he had come from moments before. The snow had caught the country by surprise and had fallen thick and fast overnight. The fall had been isolated but heavy.

A tall woman in a short blue ski jacket with square, stuffed shoulder pads walked quickly after the young boy. Her feet rising high as she followed in the deep imprints of the fleeing boy. Her expression was troubled, even from two hundred metres away the watcher could see the concern on her face.

The watcher broke his gaze and jotted something in a small notebook resting in his lap.

"Stop!" the woman shouted, her voice clear and loud and angry.

The boy disappeared into the trees just as the watcher refocussed the black military surplus optics back on the action.

The woman began to quicken her pace, her expression now melding from concern to anger as she had clearly lost sight of her quarry. The boy was no longer to be seen from the watcher's vantage point and there was no way he thought the woman would catch the little lad unless he wanted to be caught. "Come back here now, you little shit!" he heard her shout.

Standing, the watcher folded the shooting stick that he had brought to sit on and tucked it under his arm. He let the binoculars hang on the leather strap around his neck and pushed the notebook into the side pocket of his long, grey, tweed coat. He adjusted the matching trilby on his head, wrapped his grey scarf around his neck and stepped away from the edge of the ridge that overlooked the white expanse below and the action unfolding. The keys to his car jangled as he pulled them from the pocket now also occupied by the notebook and he walked quickly to the white Ford Granada parked at the end of a narrow, unmade lane.

The woman had lost the boy. She had failed. She had just one job to do and she had messed it up. He had no choice but to call it in. He had passed a red phone box a mile or so away, at the edge of a little chocolate box village, typical of this part of rural Kent. The boy would have to be found. The woman would have to go. Those were the only two options they would have. The boy could not be allowed to escape.

The watcher brushed a fresh dusting from the windscreen and threw his hat and scarf onto the backseat. He started the big car and selected reverse. He quickly turned the car at the widest part of the lane and drove quickly over the snow-hidden stones and holes as he headed back towards the road that led to the village. He'd make the call and then head back towards the forest to look for the boy himself. That was the right thing to do and it was something that would endear him to his manager – not that it mattered to him. The woman was finished, there was nothing he could do for her but at least he could come out of this smelling of roses – the hero of the day.

He glanced at the large kitchen knife resting on the front passenger seat. It had been a busy knife, a knife that was as adept at slicing and dicing flesh as it was at preparing the meat and veg for his daily meals. He had brought it with him through habit, not that he had intended to use it, not today. There was no need for it, but he felt strangely naked without it. As a child he had carried a stuffed green crocodile, a soft, cartoon croc he had chosen himself from a shelf loaded with different soft toy creatures at some animal park he had been dragged around as a child. That crock had become his friend, his confidante and his protector during the seemingly long cold nights of his childhood. He was still a child when the croc had disappeared one night, only to be replaced briefly by a knife he had grabbed from the cutlery drawer as he pursued Jeffrey the spotty twat who had stolen croc and held it above the gas flame on the large kitchen range. Jeffrey clearly thought it was a funny thing to do. Jeffrey stopped laughing as the knife was plunged into his heart time and again until the men in the white coats had pulled him from the lifeless blood-soaked body of Jeffrey the twat.

    That was a long time ago and a series of knives had replaced the croc since then. Since the arthritis began to deform his hands, he had not felt comfortable holding the blade. What had once been an extension of his hand had become a painful burden. He was tired. His purpose in life had faded. Once he had been needed, the go-to man for all kinds of things that others would never do. Now, with age came a reduction in effectiveness and therefore a reduction in perceived value to those who had handsomely rewarded him for his troubles in the past. He had never thought these days would come.

He had always believed someone, one day, would be better than him, someone who would then replace him – end his contract for good – but that day had never come. He had kept himself at the top of his game for what was now decades. Others of his age were pottering in gardens or taking painting classes to fill their days of retirement. The watcher no longer had need for money, but he worked because he hoped one day his reign would end as it should end, quickly and violently, and he couldn't think of a better way for it to do so.

The watcher parked between cars a hundred yards from the phone box. He never locked the Granada; it was another habit. He had almost died once because he had lost his keys momentarily when he had desperately needed to flee the scene of a brutal encounter. He would never be caught out again.

He had not bothered with his hat and scarf; he had no intention of staying out in the cold for any longer than necessary. He dialled the number he had memorised over a decade ago and quickly updated the woman on the other end of the line. She had said nothing other than acknowledge she had heard the message. The watcher hung up and walked back towards his car. He would find the lad and make things right. The little bastard would have a real bollocking, but that was nothing new. He might well be young, but he had to realise he had responsibilities. He had to realise he was different.

The watcher pushed the ignition key into the lock and turned over the engine. It fired and idled as he checked his mirror to pull out of the line of parked cars. Then he noticed it. The knife had gone. Someone had stolen it. He switched off the engine. He had to find it. It was *his* knife. No one had the bloody right to steal *his* knife.

He opened the door but went no further. He felt the blade run across his neck and saw his blood spurt from his severed carotid artery. He knew he was dead but he had to see who had finally managed to do what so many others had failed to do. He turned to peer into the back seat then began to laugh. He dropped out of the car onto the snow. Spurts of crimson created a macabre Jackson Pollock on the virgin powder. He saw the boy, the boy with the ever so slight limp climb out of the back door and smile down at him. The watcher's knife was in the boy's hand, hanging at his side. The boy watched the watcher, fascinated by the sight, the horror he had created. He smiled and then the watcher laughed as his life quickly drained along with his blood.

Future's Past by David j Henson

## JANUARY 2019.

It was the look of horror on the faces of children that hurt him most. They were innocent and reacted to the sight in the most natural of ways – basic instinct. He didn't blame them; he felt the same way. They had never seen anything like him before. The children had probably been read stories of beasts and monsters lying in wait beneath their beds and he truly understood their reaction towards him. It was the sneers and looks of disgust from the parents and others who should have known better that really angered him. Did they really think he *wanted* to look like this? Occasionally, there would be genuine expressions of sympathy, but he had never wanted that either. He just wanted to be left alone, to be ignored, to blend into the crowd; just like he had done before. He had never been anything other than average; average looks, average build, average height. The only thing above average was his intelligence. His parents were owners of a small cinema in London and they had been amazed how, at a young age, he could memorise most of the words from any film he had watched. They had never wanted him to follow them into the business. His sister was seemingly earmarked for that role. Rather than follow his parents into the cinema business, he had forged his own career, a decision that would ultimately lead him to this place and time. Fate had promised so much but delivered so little. He had been successful in his chosen career, he had gained promotion and even settled down with a woman he loved dearly – even though they had both never wanted to marry. Then things changed in the blink of an eye. Life would never be the same again. His fiancé had left, along with the money he had saved for a rainy day and, whilst he had every right to chase her through the courts to recover that money, he had decided she deserved it. She had put up with the unsocial hours, the bad moods, the tempers, the nightmares and the broken promises that were common within the job. He would have done the same, had he been her. What woman would want to be seen with him now? He had rarely felt sorry for himself during the first weeks and months of recovery. There was always hope but he was also a realist and the last twelve months had taken their toll. He was not going to improve any further. He was a monster.

    John Wise climbed the stairs to his apartment on the third floor of his apartment block and entered the pristine flat. He pulled the small plastic case from his coat and broke the cellophane seal. He slipped the DVD disc into his player and used the remote to run the film. He had always loved going to the movies.

Ever since he was a child, he had been fascinated by the movie theatres, the experience of buying sweets and popcorn, a soft drink and then two hours of entertainment, an escape into a world of make-believe. The cinema had always been a sanctuary to him and his family. Movies had always helped him to forget the bad dreams, the dreams he couldn't explain, the dreams that tormented and terrified him. They were nearly always the same and he desperately wanted them to end. They played out like sick movies, like the so-called snuff movies of the past that seemed to portray him as the evil antagonist. Were they portents of a grim future that had now become a reality, an insight to the monster he had now become?

    Whenever he had problems he'd head straight to the cinema. He desperately wanted to go there again but had been reduced to watching new films on disc. It wasn't the same, but it still gave him some respite from the reality of his life. He promised himself he'd return to the local cinema one day but there were bridges that had to be rebuilt before that day came.

## **NOVEMBER 2019**

## CHAPTER 1

A fine mist of smoke enveloped the bouncing bodies packed into the dimly lit nightclub. The techno music demanding a rhythm the dancers were obediently matching on the crammed dancefloor.

A smartly dressed man pushed his way through the revellers at the fringe of the melee towards the brightly lit bar spanning the entire wall at the furthest end of the club. No one paid him any real attention, just the occasional glance as he squeezed past, the occasional nod, or smile, or frown at his fleeting presence.

He had a target, a focus for his energy.

A young woman sat alone at the bar, perched upon a tall bar stool, turned towards the dancers, her head bobbing slightly in time with the thumping bass line, sipping the last dregs of her tall glass of clear alcohol. He had timed it right. She would finish her drink just as he would reach her. Perfect.

"A gin and tonic for me and whatever this lady is drinking," the man shouted to the barman as he squeezed alongside the young woman.

"That's nice of you," she shouted back over the music. She smiled. He could see the haze of alcohol clouding her pretty brown eyes. She was perfect.

Petite, blonde hair short and styled into tight curls that framed her well defined features. Her bright red lipstick matched the colour of her short, clinging dress and her breasts were well proportioned – not too big and not too small – perfect. He leaned close to her and inhaled deeply, absorbing her aroma.

The blonde leaned away, unsure at first of the unusual action of the stranger, then smiled.

"I'll have the same as you," she added. This time the smile was warm with a clear hint of interest in the tall, good-looking man standing next to her. He was her type after all. She preferred tall men. Her perfect man would also need to be sporty looking, someone who looked after himself, someone who cared about their appearance. This guy ticked all the boxes.

The man had a warm smile, a confident expression that should have set off warning sirens in Cindy's head, but she had always been a sucker for bad boys too. He was a player. Probably used to getting his way with women. He had 'come and get me' written all over him and she guessed there were few women who would refuse his hypnotic gaze.

He paid for the drinks and handed a glass to Cindy. She watched him carefully. She knew about the Rohypnol that some bastards would slip into drinks to get their way with women, but the man made no attempt to distract her as he handed her the glass. He probably knew he didn't have to drug a girl to have his wicked way with her, not with those dark, sultry looks. His hair was not long but was well cut and whatever product he used was shining on his wavy locks. He reminded her of that actor off Poldark – he was a snack, for sure.

Poldark held out his hand. "Isaac. Pleasure to meet you."

The smile, the white, even teeth. Perfect.

Cindy returned the smile with her own perfect version. "Cindy, like the doll but absolutely no plastic and far more intelligent."

Isaac laughed. "I suppose it's appropriate for such a doll of a woman," he said, then held up his hand to stop her reply. "I know, cheesy and I guess you've heard it before?"

She laughed. "Curse of the name."

"Come here often?" he said, then laughed again.

He had a nice laugh, she thought, natural, easy, his eyes laughed too. That was good. "Got a taste for cheese, have you?"

He nodded as he took a sip from his glass. "Only the smooth, spreadable kind."

"Prefer mine hard," she grinned wickedly.

\*\*\*

It had rained all day but at least it had stopped now, for a while, and that was a blessing. Sleeping rough in the winter was something Tom Purdue would never get used to. He had accepted his situation many years ago but that didn't make it any easier.

Tom had been a clever child. His parents had both been doctors, and both pushed him towards achieving his potential in school, something he did without really trying. He had stayed on and achieved three A-grades in mathematics, physics and biology. The future had looked bright. An offer to study medicine at university was a given and Tom had looked forward to the student life. That was until that fateful night in 1990 when his parents didn't return from a trip to the theatre. The police officers who called at the detached house in Beckenham were kind and considerate, but no words of comfort could help him deal with the loss of both parents that night. Hit by a stolen taxi being driven by a drunk kid, both his parents were killed instantly.

That one devastating instant had destroyed Tom. It had robbed him of his parents and any motivation to start university a month later. He found solace in a bottle of cider and soon it became two and then three. Then, when the cider no longer helped him escape his feelings of loss and despair, the cider was replaced with vodka and gin or whiskey or, when the money ran out, any cheap spirit.

His parents had left the house to him in their will and a modest inheritance but that had been whittled away in less than a year. Unable to work, Tom sold the house and moved into a rented flat for a year until he had spent the money he had left. He knew there were benefits he could tap into from the social services, but Tom was ashamed of himself. The sense of guilt associated with his behaviour sent him spiralling down even further and he was left with no option than to sleep on the streets.

Snacking on a sandwich donated by a passer-by, Tom walked slowly along the high street towards the alley he had used as shelter from the worst of the weather for over a month. It had been a good place to bed-down. There was a dumpster in the alley and that had served as temporary accommodation in the first week, but he had narrowly avoided being picked up and dumped into the back of the rubbish crusher and now slept behind the big, green plastic bin.

***

Cindy held Isaac's hand as he led her through the dancefloor towards the exit. What the hell was she doing? She had only just met him and here she was leaving the club with him. He was the smoothest guy she had ever met but it was his smile that had sealed the deal for her. No man with a smile like Isaac's could be anything other than genuine. He was the full package and she silently berated herself for desperately wanting to see what else the package offered.

The November rain had stopped as they stepped out into the street. Isaac put his arm around her waist and kissed her gently on her forehead. Cindy stopped and turned into him. "This is crazy. We've only just met."

Isaac smiled. "Don't worry. I just want to spend some time with you. We'll find somewhere quite for a drink and a chat so you can tell me all about yourself."

"And here was I thinking you just wanted to fuck me," she laughed.

Isaac shrugged. "Well, I have to admit that it did cross my mind." He nodded towards a narrow lane between a line of high street shops opposite the club. "Come on."

Cindy grinned and giggled like a drunken schoolgirl as he led her into the alley and behind a large dumpster outside a metal service door for one of the shops.

Isaac pushed her gently into the wall as he began to smell her again, like a ravenous animal checking the condition of the meat he was about to devour. Cindy giggled and shivered as he began to kiss her with a passion she had not felt since Dave. Dave had been her first true love, a boy she had met in her last year of secondary school, a boy who looked like he would grow into the perfect specimen she had pictured as her ideal man. They had been kids, but the passion had been as mature and fulfilling as anything she had ever experienced since, until now.

Cindy let Isaac take the lead. He caressed her breasts as she let the cold brick wall support her. Her legs trembled with the cold and Isaac had picked up on it. His hand slipped down to her thigh and began to rub gently between her legs. She could feel his excitement pressing up against her and, whilst she had no intention of making love in a dirty, dark alleyway, that didn't mean they couldn't have a bit of fun. She let her own hand slip down his back and around to the front of his trousers. She gasped as she felt him. He was certainly pleased to see her. She grinned to herself as he continued to kiss her. She felt his hand move up from her legs and could hear him fishing for something in his pocket. Probably well prepared with condoms, she thought, but there would be no need for them. She was on the pill, had been since Dave, but there would be plenty of time for sex. Tonight was too soon to go all the way and it was far too cold for that anyway. She was about to say no when his hand rose to her breasts again and then up to her neck. She felt his hand travel quickly from left to right below her chin and then felt something warm running down her breasts. She felt no pain, nothing. Then she pulled away from Isaac and looked down at the blood pumping from her throat.

"What... what have you...?" she screamed as she realised she had made a mistake, a fatal mistake.

***

The sandwich had been ~~okay~~OK – beggars really couldn't be choosers – ham and cheese had never been Tom's first choice of a filling, but he was grateful for anything he could get. He was still hungry, his stomach growled in protest at the lack of sustenance, but there was little chance of adding to its contents tonight. He needed to sleep. He saw the nightclub opposite his alley and knew some late-night dancers liked to top-up with a kebab or something similar on their way home. The bins around the alley often turned up the odd discarded morsel. He checked the bin outside the club but there was nothing more than cigarette butts and some empty fast-food wrappers that stank. His stomach rumbled once more but it looked like he was out of luck. Tomorrow was another day. He headed across the road towards the alley. He always stopped and checked the place before entering the dark, narrow street. He could hear something ahead, near the dumpster. It sounded like an injured cat, a shuffling and pitiful mewing.

He walked slowly towards the sound. The pitiful sounds continued as he approached. He dreaded what he might find but knew he couldn't walk away. He loved animals, always had and saw the creatures that occupied the streets at night as soul mates. He just hoped there would be something he could do to help. As he stepped around the large dumpster, he screamed at the sight of the young woman lying on the wet ground. Her throat had been cut and her dress slit from the cleavage down to her abdomen. He shook his head, refusing to believe the sight his eyes perceived. He knelt down alongside the poor woman. The blood was everywhere, and he knew there was little he could do to help her other than call for an ambulance. He stood quickly, just as a dark figure stepped out from the doorway behind the poor woman. He saw the blade in the man's hand and froze. He wanted to run but his legs refused to respond.

## CHAPTER 2

One of the wheels squeaked annoyingly as Martha Bowles pushed the handcart along the plush pale blue carpet towards the next room on her list. She had asked the caretaker to oil the damned thing, but nothing got done these days unless a customer complained. Four rooms done and another dozen to go. The wheel would have to be oiled or replaced. The manager would go nuts if a customer did complain about the noise. It wasn't loud but it was certainly enough to be heard inside the rooms. The hotel prided itself on cleanliness and made a big deal out of the spotless facilities they provided wealthy guests. It rankled with her that they needed her to maintain the high standards they expected but still only paid her the minimum wage. She was indispensable but no one seemed to value her. They could stuff their job. She had been offered a position with another hotel, a rival chain just a mile away, with the promise of an extra two pounds per hour for her services. Martha wasn't comfortable with change. She liked things to be predictable but enough was enough.

The door to room 213 was a clone of all the others along the corridor and identical to all the other doors on all the other floors. It was as if some mad scientist had genetically engineered the hotel. She had lost count of the number of times a guest had got lost with no distinguishing fixtures or features to help them find their bearings.

She checked the door handle for the 'Do Not Disturb' sign and the electronic display on the wall next to the door. The hotel had recently fitted the displays to all the room to allow guests to touch a button inside the room to notify the cleaner if they wanted the room to be made up. There was also an option for 'Do Not Disturb' too, but the panel was illuminated with a green square, that meant there was no one inside. She slipped the plastic key card into the lock of door 213 and called out just in case there was someone still there. No reply. She hauled the heavily laden trolley after her. The room was typically large and well-appointed. This room was in a corner of the modern building and the bedroom was dog-legged from the door around to the right where the bed stood in an alcove with a bifold door beyond leading onto a large balcony. The bed would need clean sheets but there was an order of service that she never deviated from. Martha liked consistency. She never changed her routine. She pushed open the door to the bathroom. A pile of used towels was dumped in the bath and she collected then up and threw them into the large 'dirties' bag attached to the end of the trolley. Martha picked out four freshly laundered, white towels from the top of the cart and placed them with precision on the racks.

Next came the toiletries. The hotel offered only the best mini versions of a high-end range that most guests would stuff into their cases when they left. It was always the same, with few exceptions. Even though most of the guests could clearly afford the three-hundred-plus pounds per night rate, they still stole the bloody toiletries.

She squeezed past the cart into the bedroom and froze.

The bed would need more than just a change of sheets. The walls would need to be painted and even the ceiling. She thought about how someone would have to remove the blood-soaked body and who would have to clean up all that blood. At least it wouldn't be her. Then her mind seemed to slap her back to reality and she began to scream.

***

Doctor Felicity Saunders finished her coffee and stared at the screen. The data was conclusive. Her work was done. She had mixed emotions. Her contract would now be finished and, whilst she felt proud of her achievement, she dreaded the search for a new job, a new project willing to employ a geneticist. She had spent the last three years at the lab, and she had enjoyed her time there. The work was essential, and the testing had been rigorous. The results had exceeded all expectations.

She checked her watch and pressed send on to send the email posting the latest results to her line manager. The work was top-secret and everything the lab sent through the intranet was secure and encrypted with the highest levels of the latest software.

She knew she had been valued at the laboratory. The centre was dedicated to genetic research and she knew that her role was just a tiny but essential part in the study. There were many other projects being undertaken, none of which she was privy to. She rarely met any of the other doctors and technicians. They were separated by their buildings, each building had its own facilities, restaurant, bar, and other amenities designed to make each worker's time at the lab as comfortable as possible. Even the start and finish times of each lab were designed to keep everyone separate. Felicity had never been bothered by that. She understood the need for secrecy. The profits of any research facility depended upon the utmost discretion.

She packed her things, there wasn't a lot, just a photograph of her parents and some odds and ends that comfortably fitted within a small shoe box. Most of her personal belongings had been taken out over the last few weeks in expectation of this last day. She carried her box, along with her coat, out of the building and walked the hundred metres towards the car park at the side of the complex.

Felicity pressed the unlock button on her key fob and her black mini flashed its indicators to inform her of its location amongst the hundred or so other vehicles in the car park. She opened the door and slipped behind the wheel. As she closed the door, she felt a hand grab her from behind. She had no time to scream. The blade sliced through her throat easily. The door opened and the dying body was pushed out onto the tarmacadam. She was already dead when the killer began to carry out his dreadful work on her body, hidden between her car and a large S.U.V.

## CHAPTER 3

The radio began to play a new song by some male singer with adenoid problems loud enough to wake John Wise from his pleasant dream. Sleep was John's friend. He never had nightmares, which was a miracle, considering.

He threw back the bleached white bed sheet and sat on the edge of the bed for a moment, taking deep breaths before he stood slowly. His head hurt like hell, a troop of military drummers beating a tattoo within his skull. It had been a heavy night, the empty bottle of vodka lying next to his feet on the thick pile carpet evidence of his drunken dive into oblivion. He rarely drank alcohol; he had made a resolution never to rely on it. But last night had been the third anniversary of the day that changed his life. The drink had helped him sleep, to escape from the reality of his life, a life that had become seriously fucked-up.

He walked in just his shorts to the radio alarm next to the door. He had deliberately placed the thing near the door to ensure he had to get out of bed to switch it off, a habit he had formed when he had first joined the job over twenty years ago. It was a habit that he hadn't thought of breaking even though he no longer needed to get up. He was a creature of habit, he had realised many years before that he had an addictive personality, but that demon had never truly possessed him until the months following the incident. The need for cleanliness to prevent infection had turned into an obsession. He pressed the off switch on the top of the radio, but the nasal singer continued to torment him, He grabbed at the box and ripped it from the socket and threw it onto the bed.

He opened the door to the kitchen diner and entered a space that would grace any ideal homes magazine. The units were clear, each worktop appliance had its own place to be stored and the granite worktop was polished to a sheen. The white grout between the wall and floor tiles looked as fresh and bright as the first day it was applied and the carpet in the sitting area still had the fresh aroma of the day it was laid. Wise knew his addiction to cleaning was part of his O.C.D. but he hated a mess. He took a glass from the orderly rows within a wall cupboard and a newly pressed dishcloth from a drawer. He wiped the glass and poured a shot of orange juice. He checked the depth of the liquid in the glass; three fingers. He had perfected the pour.

Slumping in front of the sixty-inch television set, he balanced the glass on the arm of the chair and fished the remote from a chair-tidy Darla had bought for him. He pressed the on-button, but nothing happened. He cursed and prised the bottom off the battery compartment and rolled the batteries in their housing in the hope of warming them up to squeeze some extra life out of them. He pressed the button again and the television clicked into life.

He scrolled through channels and stopped on a twenty-four-hour news station. He recognised the face staring back it him. It was a face that had not experienced the things he had experienced. It was a face that showed confidence, a face that was experienced and ambitious. It was a face that had once stared back at him in the bathroom mirror but a face that no longer resembled him in his present state. He fumbled the remote as he switched off the set.

Wise felt the anger rise deep inside him, the furious magma bursting through the rocks of an active volcano. He remembered what the psychiatrist had said about controlling the outbursts. Square breathing. He had never found it of any use. He grabbed the juice and took a long gulp. The orange liquid rained down onto the lava, temporarily quenching the fury. He drained the glass and returned to the kitchen where he poured another, four-finger shot of orange. A knock at the door halted the glass at his lips.

"John?"

"Shit!" Wise recognised the voice.

"John, come on, for fuck sake, open the door."

He thought about ignoring the visitor, to finish the juice and hope his former boss would go away, but Wise knew Detective Superintendent Monroe would not go away. He had always been a tenacious bastard, ever since Wise had taken him on to the C.I.D. as a Detective Constable fifteen years ago. Monroe and Wise had risen through the ranks together. Wise had always stayed a rank above his colleague until Wise stalled at D.C.I. It had been inevitable for Wise. No officer could advance with complaints hanging over them and Wise always had a string of complaints. He didn't care. He had loved his job and did it without fear or favour. Yes, he upset people in the process, but he hadn't been in a normal job. He had dealt with shit on a daily basis and shit usually rose to the surface and coated anything floating in it. Monroe had been more diplomatic. He was a good copper, but he had always set his sights on the upper ranks of the service and soon overtook Wise. The roles had reversed but Monroe had treated his former boss with respect. That was until Wise made his final fuck- up that resulted in his present predicament.

Wise placed the glass on the carpet next to the armchair and pulled a dressing gown from a pile of ironed clothes in a plastic basket in a wall cupboard.

He pushed his arms through the sleeves and tied the gown at the waist as he walked to the door.

"Fuck off!" he shouted.

Monroe knocked again. "Come on you twat. I need to speak to you."

Wise rested his head against the door and sighed before slipping the chain and turning the lock. He cracked the door open and stood aside.

Monroe stepped inside and sniffed the air. "Jesus! This place smells like a whore's boudoir after it's been sterilised."

"Since when did whores ever sterilise and since when has cleanliness been an offence?" Wise said. "Have you come to talk or to insult me?"

"For God's sake, John. How can you live like this? This obsession is... well... obsessive."

Wise shrugged and walked back to his armchair. He slumped into the seat and picked up his glass. "You looking to rent?"

Monroe snorted. "Nothing wrong with a bit of mess, you know. Mess means you're busy. How do you find the time?"

"Don't have much else to do, do I?"

Monroe realised his mistake. "Sorry."

"Always were a callous twat."

Monroe walked around the armchair and stood in front of Wise. "Are you OK, John? Are you really happy like this?"

Wise shrugged again. "As happy as I can be, considering."

"There was a time when you'd be happy to see me."

"Yeah. There was a time when I could do the job I loved."

Monroe shook his head. "I didn't want you to go, you know that. You had a choice."

"There's never a choice for someone like me."

Monroe knew he was losing an argument that had been fought many times before over the past three years and he also knew he couldn't afford to annoy Wise any further. He needed his help. "I haven't come to argue with you."

"What have you come for?"

"I need to talk to you…"

"So you keep saying."

"Look, I'm not here to listen to your broken record."

"So, why are you here?"

"I've got a problem I need your help with."

"Go to the clinic. They'll put you on a series of antibiotics. In case it's slipped your mind, I'm no longer a copper."

"Just hear me out, OK?"

Wise held up his empty glass. "Sure you don't want a drink? It's only OJ."

"No thanks."

"~~Okay~~OK, I'm listening."

Monroe began to pace the floor in front of Wise, clearly searching for the right words. Conflicted: but knowing he had no other option. "Two words. Serial killer."

Wise snorted. "If this is another one of your 'let's get John back into the fold' tricks, you can forget it. Even if I wanted to, you'd find resistance in the nick."

"Don't flatter yourself. If you want to lock yourself away that's up to you. I, on the other hand, have a more pressing problem to deal with. For God's sake John, one mistake in nearly thirty."

"And what a fucking beauty, eh?"

"Please, John. This life... it's not normal."

Wise ran a finger around the rim of his glass and then spoke. "Fuck you! Just get out."

"What happened, John? You were a good copper. Now look at you. You're a fucking joke. This pains me to ask... I've got Rickett breathing down my neck, eager to take the case and he's the last fucker I want involved. And, I don't want to give you the chance to tell me to fuck off again, but... truth is, I need your help. There was no one better than you at this shit."

"What about Krosonofski, he's a good man. Why not get him on the case?"

Monroe nodded. "He's a good man but I need your help with the profiling. Will you just hear me out?"

Wise sighed and waved a hand. "Fine."

"~~Okay~~OK. Yesterday, the body of a young woman was found in the car park of the Innovations lab just out of town."

"I know where the lab is," Wise said tersely. "It's that research centre."

Monroe nodded.

"Yeah, anyway, as soon as we began to investigate the death we were shut down. Order came from above."

"How far above?"

"I don't know. It must have been pretty high up. Well above my pay scale."

"Only the Commissioner could pull that one."

"Or the Deputy?"

Wise nodded.

"All I know is that the Commander was called to a meeting and the plug was pulled."

"I get it. Your hands are tied so you want someone on the outside to poke around and do your dirty work and take the fall if it all goes tits up. Am I wrong? Tell me I'm wrong," he grinned sarcastically.

Monroe walked over to a recently cleaned window, he could smell the Windolene, and stared at the scrap yard opposite Wise's flat. "I can't. You're right. I managed to pull a few strings and got a look at the file and the autopsy report. It seems the lab murder was not the first. Two others have been killed in the last three days. A woman in a hotel and a vagrant in an alley opposite the Harper's nightclub in town."

"You think it's the same killer?"

"Two murders were identical in every way bar one... location. The vagrant is different. Stabbed first and then had his throat cut, but the blood in the alley is not only from him. The blood in the alleyway suggests two victims and we have a missing person, a woman named Cindy Gray. I'm guessing she was killed there and then perhaps removed after the killer was disturbed by the tramp. Whoever it was knew exactly what they were doing."

"In what way?"

"The use of the blade. Precision."

"A doctor?"

"Both women had their wombs removed. One of the docs I did manage to speak to said it was a work of art, for Christ's sake."

Wise groaned and stood up from the chair. He walked to the sink and ran the tap over the glass. He wiped it clean again and filled his glass with water and took a long drink. "You think this nutter is a doctor or surgeon?"

"Could be. Truth is, I don't know. The lab probably has a surgeon and a shit load of doctors on site."

"You think someone from the lab is involved?"

"It was you that told me not to discount anything. Truth is, I don't know. I've been racking my brain for some kind of connection or some lead that will help us, but I haven't a clue. When the lab came up as a scene, I just clung to the possibility a doctor was involved but who the hell knows?"

"I also told you that the suspect that is seemingly too obvious is often the only one that matters. It's a good place to start."

"Does that mean you'll help?"

"You know I don't go out in the daylight."

"Nobody gives a shit, John. Most people around here know you."

"I don't go out in daylight," he said sternly.

Wise returned to his chair and sat once more. Monroe followed like a loyal puppy, eager to get a reward. Wise forced a fake and disfigured smile. "Hell, it's not like I've got shit else to do. What will I get paid?"

Monroe looked embarrassed. "Nothing officially. I can get some money~~paid~~ from the department nark fund but..."

"The nark fund?"

"It's all I can do."

"I need to see everything you have."

"It's not a lot but I'll get it to you on the Q.T."

"I guess that will have to do."

\*\*\*

Wise ran the shower – cold – and stood under it until his head cleared. Hot showers had become a thing of the past. He shaved the one side of his face that still had follicles and slipped into one of his old suits he hadn't worn since he had been forced out of the police. He wiped a dry cloth over his head and winced at the pain that still took him by surprise and stared at his reflection. He flinched at the sight. The skin on the right side was tight and puckered, red raw and sore from the dozens of grafts he had undertaken since the acid had been thrown in his face. His right eye had lost the bright blue colour Darla had loved; now it was a milky white. His hair had gone with the liquid and would never grow back. His lips had escaped the damage and he was grateful for that, at least the beast could kiss his beauty if he ever found her. He checked his pockets and found the stub of a cigarette. How did he forget that? He tossed it in the waste bin and sprayed his suit with a cheap aftershave he had received from his sister at Christmas.

He ~~thought about~~ considered taking his car but thought better of it. The last thing he needed was to lose his license. He hadn't driven since the attack and he doubted the old Jeep would even start. He called a taxi and took the ride to the café where Monroe had told him he'd meet him. He ignored the expected stares and ordered a strong black coffee and waited for Monroe to arrive.

The Detective Superintendent arrived twenty minutes later and waved away the waitress.

"I take it you'll stand me another coffee?" Wise grinned.

Monroe sighed and dropped a thick folder wrapped in a Tesco carrier bag onto the table. "Take a look and I'll get the coffee."

Wise removed the file and liberated it from the thick rubber band keeping the contents inside. He scanned through the pages before Monroe returned with his coffee.

"What do you think?"

"Give me a chance. I've only just flicked through it."

"I know you, John. You've probably seen all you need to see."

Wise took a sip of the coffee and nodded. "I've seen enough from the autopsies to know you've got a serial killer, for sure."

"Doesn't take a fucking genius."

"I need to check out the scene."

"That could be awkward."

"Do you want me to help you or not?"

"Of course I do…"

Wise took another sip and stared at Monroe. He wiped a tear from his damaged eye.

"~~Okay~~OK. I'll take you there as soon as you finish that."

\*\*\*

"Got to stop off at the office, check with the team. Arranged a briefing. I want you to come in so I can update them with your involvement. I don't want any of the buggers spouting off to the top brass. Forewarned, and all that bollocks."

Wise shouted. "Stop the car, now!"

Monroe ignored him.

"Stop the car now. I'm warning you. There's no way I'm going back in there."

"Time you faced the old crew, John. Can't keep hiding forever."

"Yes, I can. Now stop the car or I'll open this door and jump out." He heard the deadlocks engage but hadn't seen Monroe press the button on his door. "That's fucking childish."

"Me, childish? You're a good one talking."

Wise sighed, resigned to being trapped. "I can't," he said quietly. "I can't."

"You can and you will."

They sat in silence for the rest of the journey and only spoke again as the car pulled through the security gate at the rear of the station. "OK, here we are then. I sometimes think I know this place better than my home."

Wise said nothing.

Monroe turned in his seat to face him. "Come on. It'll only take half an hour, tops."

Monroe smiled but Wise didn't smile back. He heard the lock click and opened the door. "On your head be it," Wise warned.

Leading the way, Monroe used his ID card to enter the station through the charge room entrance with Wise following behind.

The charge room sergeant, a grizzled twenty-five-year veteran, looked up from his desk at the new arrivals. "Who've you got for me…" he began to say then froze, his expression morphing from curiosity to stunned anger. "What the fuck is he doing here? I hope you've nicked the twat?"

Monroe stopped at the desk. "Enough, Dave, he's with me."

Dave the sergeant stood slowly from his chair and towered over Monroe and Wise.

"You'd better sit again, Dave, you know that if we go toe-to-toe there's only going to be one walking out in one piece and that sure as fuck isn't going to be you," Wise growled.

"You think so?"

"I know so. You've always been a fucking bully, that's why you're in here and not retiring in five years as an inspector."

The sergeant's face flushed red. "I don't care if you are with the guvnor, I'm going to rip your face off… what's left of it," he added.

Wise smirked. "Don't let my good looks put you off. Anytime, you giant piece of shit."

Dave stepped out from behind the desk, but Monroe stepped between him and Wise. "You stand down, Dave or I swear I'll put you on the book." He turned to Wise, "And you can stop winding him up too..."

Wise held up his hands and grinned. "I told you I didn't want to be here."

Big Dave stood aside and let the two men pass. "You'll get what's coming to you, Wise. You're not one of us anymore and I'm just at the front of a long queue waiting for a chance to put you out of your misery."

"One more fucking word out of you and I'll have your stripes," Monroe hissed.

"You need to pick your friends more carefully... SIR," Dave said, ironically emphasising the honorific.

The team of detectives were already gathered in the briefing room when Monroe and Wise walked in. They stood as their boss entered and then several began to moan about Wise's presence. Monroe held up his hand.

"~~Okay~~OK, shut up and sit down. John is here to help us. He's volunteered his expertise and I, for one, am happy he's here. If any of you have a problem with that you can leave right now. But, be warned, if you walk out now you won't be coming back as a detective."

It was clear to Monroe that several of his team were considering the ramifications of protesting the presence of their former boss but none of them took action. They sat and stared at Wise as he leaned against a wall near the front.

The room doubled as a CID office, one end was fitted out with desks and computers and a smaller area had been left clear for briefings. A large glass screen was illuminated with L.E.D's from below for the briefing officers to write with dry-wipe markers that glowed in the light. Monroe began the briefing and scribbled the names of the known victims and then wrote the name of the missing woman and circled it several times. "So, this is a serious worry. We have one possible victim… actually I'd say 'probable' victim we haven't found yet. She has to be our priority just in case the killer is still holding her as hostage. If there's any chance she's still alive then we have to act fast and find her. Like I say, she's probably already dead but whilst there's the slightest chance she isn't, we treat her as an abduction."

"What help is Wise going to be, sir?" a young detective asked. The sarcasm in his tone wasn't lost on Monroe but he let it go.

"John, as you know, brought to justice some of the worst serial killers this force has ever dealt with. There is no one better versed at getting inside the heads of killers."

"Takes one to know one, guv," another detective pitched in.

Wise grinned then stepped forward. "I know you don't want me here. I don't want to be here either, but I've been asked to help and that's what I'm doing. I can't undo the past, but if I can do anything to catch this killer then I will. You don't have to like me, but I always thought you were all professionals, God, I even took most of you on as detectives. So, for the next few days or weeks, all I ask is that you focus your anger for me towards finding this killer. When he's caught, if you still want a pop at me, I'll stand here and let you."

More murmuring, then a man stood at the front. He nodded at Wise. "What you did left a sour taste in our mouths, guv, but I know you were a shit hot detective and you always treated us all with respect. For that much, I'm prepared to put aside our differences for the time being, but I'll be at the front of the queue to take that pop at you when this is all over."

Wise nodded. "Then, what's your take on these killings, Bert?" Wise asked.

## CHAPTER 4

His personal best was improving rapidly. Just the thick end of a five-minute mile was still impressive, and Isaac was pleased. He had always kept himself fit, ever since he was a child and he was born blessed with an abundance of fast-twitch muscle fibres that made him the fastest child at school. School had been fun, but it had been a strange school and all the better for that strangeness. Isaac had loved his time with the other kids. They were all like him, talented, bright and each possessed some innate gift other children in ordinary schools didn't. In a place where everyone was different, Isaac was even more exceptional, at least that's what he had always believed. Isaac possessed most of the gifts of the others. He was truly blessed. It had been like the X-Men without the fancy costume and pants outside the trousers.

Hardly out of breath, Isaac dropped to the grass at the side of the path that wound through the park and pushed out fifty press-ups. He loved the buzz from physical exertion and knew his passion for exercise bordered on an addiction. He had an addictive personality, but, unlike others with the same propensities, Isaac had avoided drugs. Drugs were the scourge of humankind. They created flaws that were often fatal and reduced people to a shadow of their true capabilities. Isaac hated weakness. Weakness was a curse, a plague that had no place on earth. Survival of the fittest.

He rolled over onto his back and stared at the sky. The clouds were dark and heavy, full of rain that he knew would soon be dumped on the world below. He didn't mind the rain. Indeed, the rain kept the little people off the streets. The rain gave him space to roam unnoticed. He thought about the school and how they would not recognise him now, even his name had changed. Isaac was the perfect name, a name that had meaning, a meaning that only he was privy to. He thought it suited him perfectly in his new life. He quickly completed a set of fifty sit-ups and sprang to his feet. He felt good, so good. He set off at a fast pace and headed for the park exit that led onto Kennington Road.

\*\*\*

Wise lit a cigarette and took two lungsful of the smoke as he walked towards the nightclub. A Police vehicle was still parked outside the entrance – a fully marked four-door Ford. He could see the uniformed officer standing at the entrance to the lane; blue and white tape strung across the entrance. He ignored the club and walked across the road to the uniform constable. As he approached, the constable raised his hand, then recognised Wise.

"Er, sorry, sir, I mean, Mister Wise. I'm afraid you're not authorised…" before he could finish his sentence, Monroe appeared behind Wise and waved the constable aside.

"Don't log Mr Wise's attendance at the scene. No mention of him in your log, you understand me?" Monroe warned him.

"Er, yes, sir, I mean no, sir."

Monroe walked beside Wise as they ducked beneath the tape and strolled towards the blood-stained dumpster. "I think this'll interest you."

"If it doesn't, I can always go home."

Monroe stopped and stared at Wise.

"I'm kidding. What's happened to your sense of humour?" Wise said.

"There's nothing funny about this shit, John."

Wise nodded. "Never is. So, what's the score?"

"About three nill, possibly four, with time on the clock slipping away," He sighed, "we've got a report of a male in mid-thirties seen with the missing woman in the club. No positive ID but it's something, I suppose. Cindy Gray, aged twenty-nine from Streatham."

Wise stepped towards the blood stains on the wall and floor.

"What do you see?" Monroe asked.

Wise pointed to the blood behind the dumpster. This is a major blood loss. It's distinct from the other large pool where I assume you found the tramp, so, I think you're right. Two victims, not one."

The constable approached. "Sir, there's a telephone call for you."

"I've got to take this. I'll check back with you later."

Wise nodded as Monroe produced the evidence file from his coat and handed it to him without the uniform seeing. "I know I don't need to remind you to keep that to yourself?"

"I'll read it in full tonight and get it back to you tomorrow."

"No copies, OK?"

"As you said, no need to remind me."

***

There was no sign of Monroe returning. Wise had taken snaps of the scene on his mobile phone and there wasn't anything else he could do that the forensics team hadn't done. He had walked the alley three times, searching for anything that might have been overlooked by the officers. He checked through the dumpster, but the contents had already been removed, probably bagged and tagged by the search team. He needed to speak to the witnesses but had to be careful. The shit would hit the fan if anyone objected.

He nodded to the uniform as he left the alley and strolled across the nightclub. He had been there a few times over the years as a customer. It had been a popular haunt for local officers during the nineties, but he had stopped going when the clientele had seemed to prefer music that sounded all the same to his ear. Wise had loved the sounds of the eighties and nineties and just couldn't understand the techno shit the club were now blasting out of their disco. Were these places even called disco's anymore? Wise didn't think so. He had no idea what the kids called these places these days. He was an analogue dinosaur living in a digital age and he didn't like it.

The double doors were open, but a hand-written sign attached to a glass pane stated the forthcoming gig had been cancelled. It was early in the day and Wise expected to see a cleaner going about his or her business. He stepped through the door into the foyer and passed the ticket counter on his left. He pushed through to the dancefloor. Another woman was polishing the floor with a large electric polisher. A woman was busy behind the bar, re-stocking the bottles of spirits on stands.

Wise walked across the dancefloor to the bar and tapped the counter for attention.

The woman turned and winced at the sight of his face. "Sorry, we're closed."

"I know, I'm with the police," he said, truthfully but bending it as far as he dared.

"You're a copper?"

"Used to be until this," he smiled his lopsided smile and pointed to his face. "I'm a consultant, ex-detective. I might look like shit, but I can still think," he added.

The woman nodded and made an apologetic shrug. "I've already spoken to the other coppers. I didn't see anything. I wasn't working that night."

"Who was it that told my colleagues he had seen the woman with a man?"

She shrugged. "I dunno. Ask your mates."

"I will but I need to speak to whoever it was urgently."

The woman sighed and crossed her arms defensively. "I guess it was Pete. Pete was here that night. He never misses a trick."

Wise jotted down the address for Pete that the girl gave him and smiled. "And finally, may I speak with the manager?"

She nodded and stepped out of the bar through a door to Wise's left. A short, rotund man, aged about forty, with a high forehead and complexion that reminded Wise of a vampire, came through the bar door and stood before him. Wise guessed the guy spent most of his time like a nocturnal creature, sleeping during the day and awake at night.

The manager stopped in his tracks at the sight of Wise, no attempt to hide his shock at the damage to his face. "Jesus! What the fuck happened to you?"

Wise shrugged. "Run the shower too hot this morning."

The man didn't know what to say, he finally nodded and spoke. "I'm the manager, Simon Devereaux. Can I help you?" the man said sternly, clearly not happy to be bothered. Wise thought he picked up a west country accent.

"I hope so. I'm trying to establish who might have seen the girl with a the man on the night she went missing."

"Cindy?"

"You knew her?" Wise was surprised.

"Aye, I know her, we all do. Regular, she is. Lovely girl. I hope nothing bad has happened to her."

"I'm hoping the same, but we have to cover all bases. Did you see her that night?"

"Yes, I saw her. She was sitting there at the bar," he pointed to a stool to Wise's right. Never saw her with anyone though. I heard Pete saw some smooth twat chatting her up, but I didn't. I gave a copy of the CCTV to your colleagues."

"Do you have the original?"

"Aye, I'll take you to the office and you can check for yourself."

Wise followed the manager up a metal staircase to a suite of offices above the dancefloor. One office was smaller and contained a large television monitor connected to the club's CCTV system. Devereaux checked through the list of stored files and clicked the mouse on the one he wanted. "I'll get us a coffee, this might take some time." Wise smiled and nodded as he took a seat in front of the screen.

\*\*\*

"It's my decision, sir," Monroe said, barely able to control his anger. "I'm responsible for this and I'll accept the consequences."

"Too fucking true, you will," the Assistant Commissioner replied tersely. "I told you to pull the plug on the lab death. I'm reliably informed that the Ministry of Defence ~~(M.O.D.)~~ are going to being dealing with it and we have had orders from the Home Secretary to stand down. Then, you can imagine~~e~~ my total fucking embarrassment when I'm told by my source that you've got John Wise, a retired invalid to act as a consultant. Does that mean you're incapable of doing the work yourself?"

Monroe bristled at the offensive word to describe his old friend. He wanted to tear into his boss but thought better of it. "No, sir."

"Well that's what it looks like and that's what it'll look like when you come to have your next fucking staff appraisal."

"Sir, Wise is helping, that's all. He's the expert with serial killers; what he doesn't know isn't worth knowing. He arrested the Sceptre." The Sceptre had plagued the southern counties of England for nearly a decade before Wise cracked the case. The killer had been a Lay Preacher – a pillar of the community who had travelled the counties killing at his leisure.

"I know all about Wise. I know he fucked-up the incident at the bank, got acid in his face for his troubles."

Monroe sighed. "Yes, sir. It was devastating."

"Then I don't have to tell you how embarrassing this will be if the press get a hold of it?"

"No, sir, but... aren't we trying to show everyone the police as an equal opportunities employer?"

"Don't be fucking smart. You know that's for L.Y.B.G.T. and people of ethnic origins."

"I think it's L.G.B.G.T-*plus*, sir."

"Whatever. So, no buts, Monroe. This is a fuckup and I want Wise out of there."

"Why would the M.O.D. be involved?"

"I have no idea. Our's isn't to question the orders of the Home Secretary. We do what we are told."

"If the M.O.D. is involved then it suggests to me the government is up to its eyes in this somehow."

"That's an assumption based on nothing. The M.O.D. run the place and that means they have control when it comes to shit like this. Remember that it's our government who pays our wages."

"But we all swore to uphold the law without fear or favour, sir. I don't give a shit about the government. We have three murders, possibly four, and we are being told to back off. This stinks."

Silence for a moment before the Deputy Commissioner replied. "Look, Monroe, I agree. My hands are tied. I've given the other murders to Rickett. He's acting up as D.C.I. for the duration and you stand down and have nothing more to do with it.

If you disobey that order and I don't find out, then I can't be held responsible, can I? It's on your head. Are you willing to risk your career for this?"

Monroe ended the call. "Shit!"

***

Wise sipped the coffee as the manager scrolled through the recording for the date in question. Six cameras had eyes on the dancefloor and bar, and one had a clear shot of Cindy sitting on the barstool.

"That's it, stop!" Wise shouted as he saw a smartly dressed man walk up to the bar and order a drink.

The manager pressed pause.

"Scroll on a little. Let's see if we can get a shot of his face."

The camera angle wasn't good. The best shot came when the man turned to talk to Cindy but only a partial profile was visible. "That's no good. Can I see the other shots for the other cameras? Perhaps we'll get him walking in or out?"

They spent a further thirty minutes going through all the available and relevant recordings and, whilst some had shots of the man, none of them had a clear image of his face.

Future's Past by David j Henson

## CHAPTER 5

Wise paid the taxi driver the fare and stepped out in front of the main gate to the Innovations Laboratory. The place was huge, a concrete and glass two-storey complex of buildings spread over what he guessed was several acres of land.

He walked up to the security box at the side of the gate and spoke to the uniformed guard. "I need to speak to the CEO or whatever the hell you call the top-dog at this place."

The guard studied Wise for a brief moment, seemingly not too bothered by what he saw. "That would be Doctor Levison."

"Then that's who I need to speak with."

"Do you have an appointment, mister...?"

"Wise. I'm with the police. I'm retired, retired Detective Inspector. I'm acting as a consultant for them."

"A consultant?"

"That's right."

"Do you have an appointment?"

"No. But I have to speak with him about the young woman..."

"I understand but I'm afraid that's being dealt with already," the guard interrupted. "I've been given orders not to speak with the police and... seeing that you're not even a real copper anymore that rules you out entirely."

"You do realise that you're obstructing police enquiries?"

"But you're not a copper and the cops have no jurisdiction here."

Wise couldn't believe his ears. "What the hell are you talking about. This is a murder enquiry and the police deal with murders. What planet are you on? How would you feel if one of your family was found in the car park with their throat cut and innards stolen and someone told you the cops weren't investigating?"

The guard shrugged. "I suppose I'd be pissed."

"Well I've never let a killer go because some bureaucrat told me to stand down. I'm going to stay here until you drag me away and then I promise it'll make the press. Imagine the shit that'll rain down on you then."

The guard was a big man but not too big. Wise had dealt with bigger men in his career and even though he was out of practice he still fancied his chances if things got out of hand. "Look. Just call Leviston..."

"Levison," the guard corrected him.

"~~Okay~~OK, call Doctor Levison and get him out here now."

The guard turned on his heel and stepped inside the box. He picked up a phone and watched Wise as he spoke. "There's a police consultant at the gate and he's refusing to leave until he speaks to Doctor Levison," he nodded once and then ended the call. "Someone will meet with you. Just wait there."

Wise lit a cigarette and had smoked three before a man in a white coat strode down the drive towards him. The gate opened and the man in the lab coat stopped, folded his arms and stared at Wise, studying his face as if he was assessing the quality of the skin grafts. A blue strap hung around the man's neck with a white plastic identity card attached to the end – probably also a security key. All places like that had card entry systems these days.

"Dr Levison?"

"Dr Levison is otherwise engaged, He's a busy man. I'm Dr Lowe."

Holding out his hand, Wise stepped towards the man and stumbled. He fell against the doctor and apologised. "Sorry, slipped," he said.

"That's OK. Now tell me what you want. I've got work to do."

"I'm here about the recent murder."

"I'm sorry, I'm sure the guard told you it's out of police hands. This is a M.O.D. investigation. We are part of the government and therefore everything comes under their remit."

"Ministry of Defence?"

"That's right. We have all received orders from them that we are not to speak to anyone about what happened here. I'm sorry." The doctor turned and walked back up the drive as the guard flicked a switch to close the gate.

The rain had started to fall as Wise checked his watch. "Shit!"

The guard stepped out of the box, but this time looked far less intimidating. "Look, you'll get soaked there. Come inside and I'll call you a taxi or, if you wait ten minutes I'll be booking off and I'll run you back into town. My name's Bob, Bob Smith."

"A lift would be great, Bob," Wise smiled. It would give him a chance to have an 'off the record' talk with the man away from his place of work.

Bob's car was a ten-year-old Nissan, it had seen better days, but Wise wasn't complaining. The rain was now lashing against the windscreen as the guard drove him into town.

"I appreciate this."

"Not a problem," the guard said. "I wanted to talk to you away from that place. I'm sorry but I couldn't speak openly back there. They have cameras and recording equipment all over the place, even infrared sensors to protect the place."

"Sounds like some seriously high security shit."

"You wouldn't believe it. They've spent more on security than we'd both earn in a couple of lifetimes."

"What do they do there?"

Bob shrugged. "Officially? Genetic research. Unofficially? I have no idea. No one seems to know." The guard took a pack of cigarettes from his coat pocket and tossed them in Wise's lap. "Help yourself and light one for me too, eh?"

Wise lit two cigarettes and handed one to Bob.

"Cheers, I needed that. Bad fucking business, this. You know, I used to be a copper. Spent ten years on the beat in the East End. Loved the job too but got into the shit over some missing person. They said I didn't follow through on the enquiry, but I did. The poor fucker turned up dead and I got the blame. It was my shift Inspector; he was to blame. I asked him to let me follow up on the report, but he said not to bother. 'She'll turn up' he said. Well, she turned up alright. Turned up in the river."

"Jesus! I'm sorry. I know how that shit goes down. Had to finish myself. Twenty-five years' service down the tube after this happened," he didn't need to point to his face, he could see Bob looking more closely at him.

"Acid?"

Wise nodded. "Bastard came up behind me. Didn't have a chance."

"Bloody hell. Now *I'm* sorry," Bob said as he took a long drag on his smoke. "I think something bad is going on at the lab. Don't ask me what but I get a bad feeling there. They've got lots of projects going on and it's all financed by some government department or other. I understand the need for secrecy in places like that, but that place is something else."

"And this Levison is in charge, you say?"

"He has been for the whole time I've been there. One of my mates said he started the place over thirty years ago but that his research goes back much further. He's must be seventy if he's a day. Looks like death warmed up and we all joke that the bastard is trying to create some elixir of life but that's just bollocks. We hardly ever see the bloke. Comes to work in a blacked out Range Rover and hardly says a word. It's not his car, they send it out to pick him up and take him home."

"I need to get inside, to take a look around."

Bob snorted. "No way. You'll never do it. Not even if I had all my mates helping. Too many security points and shit."

Wise fished in his pocket and produced a white plastic ID card on a blue sash. "That good doctor there donated this to me."

Chuckling, Bob tapped the steering wheel. "I thought I saw you take it."

"And you said nothing?"

"I'm on your side. What you said back there… about how I'd feel if it had been my relative sliced and diced. Something is going on there and someone has to find out what."

"Why haven't you done something?"

"You don't understand. This is all I've got. I have a wife and two little 'uns. I can't do something, anything that will get me sacked. And anyway, you haven't seen Big Mike."

"Big Mike? Who's Big Mike?"

"You really don't want to meet Big Mike," he sighed and shook his head. Wise noticed his knuckles turn white as he gripped the steering wheel tighter. "He's ex-S.A.S. or S.B.S. or some shit. I don't think he was – too stupid to be Special Forces. But he's hard as nails and twice as dense. A real bad bastard. He's in overall charge of security and runs the place like a fucking prison. He's one scary bugger."

"Don't fancy your chances against him, eh?" Wise grinned.

Bob looked at Wise and shook his head. "You don't understand. The guy's a psycho. He has no empathy. Never met anyone like him, even when I was a copper."

"So, whatever I do I'll have to try and avoid this Big Mike."

## CHAPTER 6

Wise needed another coffee, urgently. He felt like he needed something stronger than a coffee after what Bob had told him, but he needed a clear head. He took a table next to the window in one of the many coffee shops that had sprung up on the high street over the last few years. They were all the same, they each tried to present a different experience for their customers but essentially, they were just clones of each other, all selling the same vastly overpriced products packaged to appeal to clientele that seemed prepared to fork out more than was necessary for the convenience. Wise had never liked the places, but they had their uses – sometimes. He wiped the table with a napkin and his coffee arrived hot and black and that was all that mattered to him. He needed the caffeine kick and it certainly provided that. The waitress smiled a genuine smile and didn't seem bothered by his scars. Wise smiled back and nodded. There was nothing to say.

He thought of his plan. Big Mike was a potential problem. If Wise was ever going to get inside the Innovations Laboratory, he'd have to find a way around the man Bob had said seemed to take pride and pleasure in his heavy-handed handling of security at the lab.

He sipped his drink and wondered what had been missed by his former colleagues. He pulled the file from a deep pocket inside his overcoat and laid it out on the table. He scanned through the background information on the victims. The poor woman murdered at the lab had been a research scientist. She was clearly linked to the lab but what about the others? If someone at the lab was somehow behind the murders, there had to be a link to the other victims. The tramp could be ruled out. He was just in the wrong place at the wrong time, but Wise knew he'd have to check him too, just in case it wasn't as straightforward as it seemed. Wise had learned early on in his career that a detective could never afford to take anything for granted.

Four victims – three women and one man. Wise removed the sheets containing Tom Purdue's information. He would look at the background of the tramp later but didn't expect to find anything there that would help the investigation.

The woman killed in the hotel was Julia Johnson. Aged forty-four. She was the owner and sole operator of an Estate Agency in Clapham; a new start-up business aiming to exploit the extortionate housing market in the capitael city. She was married to Jonty Johnson – a fifty-six-year-old city financier – and they had three teenage children. A copy of her hotel booking at the hotel revealed she had booked in alone for one night. That was odd because her home was less than five miles away. Why would she be staying the night alone at a hotel when she lived so close? There were a few reasons that sprang to mind. She was perhaps meeting someone for business and expected to have too much to drink and didn't want to risk driving home. But then there was always a taxi in those circumstances. There was never a shortage of black cabs and Uber taxi's in London. The other possibility was that she was meeting someone for an illicit rendezvous. If she was having an affair, then that would make sense. He would have to check the hotel for CCTV or other single bookings. It could well be that Julia and her lover and subsequent killer booked in separately and then met up in her room where things went badly wrong for her.

Wise made a note to make enquiries at the hotel before reading the file of Cindy Gray. Gray was a twenty-nine-year-old woman from Streatham in South London. She had no next of kin and worked as a transport manager for a haulage company in Erith in Kent. Her flat had been searched by police and nothing found of interest. Her neighbours rarely saw her because she worked long hours and she had no friends listed that he could talk to. She must have friends, he thought. Everybody has someone they could call a friend, didn't they? He thought of himself. Since he lost his job none of his former colleagues had kept in touch. They had cut the ties and let him drift. It finally dawned on him that he also had no one he could call a friend. Monroe was the only former friend he had spoken to since he had finished and Monroe had only contacted him because he needed him, because he was using him.

He finished his coffee and stepped back out into the cold wet afternoon. He needed something stronger than coffee. The cases could wait until tomorrow. Today he needed escape.

*** 

The last thing Monroe had wanted to do was to call in Wise, but he had no other option he could think of. Wise was the best – had been the best detective Monroe had worked for and with. He also had a strange understanding of the minds of serial killers. He had pretty much single-handedly brought three of the psychos to justice. Wise could somehow put himself into the shoes of the killers and second-guess what they would do next. The problem with Wise was his unpredictability. No one could second-guess him. That unpredictability had eventually led to his downfall and Monroe had been instrumental in Wise's suspension and eventual 'retirement'. Monroe felt guilt but knew he had been left with no option. The decision to retire had been Wises' but had he not jumped ship he would probably have been pushed. There was no way he could continue in his present state. Now he had crawled back to the man who had mentored him through the Criminal Investigation Department and that made Monroe feel even worse. Monroe's team of detectives had gone through everything and come up with nothing. They had used Wise's own methods for detection and yet still came up dry. So why did he even think Wise could help? Had he made a mistake, a mistake that could stall his own career? Wise had become a loose cannon. Ever since that fateful day when he disobeyed a direct order and Wise's own brother-in-law ended up as a fatality, he had turned to drink in the wake of the incident and God only knew what else to block out his sense of guilt, a guilt that was justified in terms of procedure but as far as Monroe was concerned it was a guilt that would have been far worse had he not acted as he had that day.

    He poured himself a beer from the fridge and sat in his favourite armchair. He pressed play on a remote and sighed as the voice of John Miles began singing. Miles could always help ease Monroe's worries. Miles was a friend, a friend he had never met and was never likely to either, but the singer had a way of connecting to him. Monroe had already made the decision and now it was too late. Monroe was committed and Wise would have to deliver the goods. But now it had to be off the record and out of the line of sight of the Deputy Commissioner~~ACC~~ and bloody Rickett.

***

Stairway to Heaven was on repeat but not a single note registered with Wise. He lay on the bed and stared at the ceiling, watching the lines of the Artex dance and swirl, merge and disappear. He felt sick and closed his eyes, hoping the nausea would pass. He saw his sister's face as she saw her husband take the bullet to the throat. He saw her silently mouth words of hatred as Wise knelt over her husband's body trying in vain to stem the bleeding. His own face sizzled and stank as the acid ate into his face but he had not thought of himself. The pain had been horrendous, and he had poured a bottle of water over his burns with one hand as he had kept pressure on Peter's wound. "It's all your fault," she had said. Wise knew the words all too well, he'd heard them so many times from his sister and the court and Professional Standards investigators. They didn't have to tell him. He knew. But what else could he have done? His sister and her husband had been taken hostage along with a dozen others in a high street bank. The idiots with the guns were mean, seemingly with no plan and no idea of how they would get through the automated anti-holdup systems all banks now employed. They had no chance of getting away with money and no chance of escape from the police as soon as those systems had activated, and the alarm was picked up instantly at the control room. If they had just thrown down their weapons and walked out as Wise had ordered them to, then all would have ended well but one robber, a man who looked more like a movie star than a local thug, had put a gun to his sister's head. That was when Wise had acted. Against orders, he had entered under the pretence of negotiations, and it might have gone well had Wise's brother-in-law not started shooting his mouth off and winding up the hostage taker. As the thug turned his gun away from Wise's sister, and aimed it at Peter, Wise pulled his concealed weapon, a Glock, and took a shot. He found his target but not in time. The thug had squeezed off a round that would end the life of one man and end the career of Wise. Then all hell was unleashed. The remaining two robbers began firing. Wise was soaked in the acid as the youngest of the robbers, a young man he had not seen, crept up behind him and threw the liquid in his face. Three other hostages were killed in the crossfire. Wise never saw the old woman one of the rounds struck and had no idea that she lay dying as the armed response team burst into the bank and ended the siege.

It was three days before Wise saw the printed face of the old lady killed in the hold up. Her face was plastered over the front page of all the tabloids and the television news. The media smelt blood, the public demanded it, and the Professional Standards officers ensured they got it in the shape of the gravely injured Detective Inspector John Wise.

The morphine had helped with the pain and the drug induced sleep had provided escape from the reality Wise faced. That had been the start of his fall into total reliance on chemical substances. It was a habit Wise broke after months struggling with the addiction. The cold turkey had been as bad as the pain he had suffered in the attack. The pain killers had taken the place of the morphine and Wise knew he had to break that habit too, but all in good time. He rose from the bed and dropped two soluble tablets into the glass of water on his bedside table. It would take the edge off the pain, but nothing could ease the damage that had been done to his soul. He looked like a monster and the dark desire for revenge was unbearable. There wasn't an hour in the day when he didn't think about taking his revenge on the man who had destroyed his life. He pictured the young man walking free from his two-year sentence and imagined surprising him before he could react and defend himself. He thought of where he would hide in wait and of the acid he would throw into the smug face of the little bastard. The guy was no more than twenty and he had been the only one of the robbers to walk out alive – albeit under arrest. He'd probably not even thought about the life he would ruin with his savage action, but that reckless and evil act had to be accounted for. Wise could not forget or forgive. The man would have to pay for his crime.

\*\*\*

Wise parked his Jeep in a residential street a mile from the laboratory. The car had started after charging the battery for a couple of hours with a borrowed charger from a neighbour. The drive had been slow, like a newly qualified driver taking control on his own for the first time. Three years of abstinence from driving had dented his confidence almost as much as the bodywork of the old Jeep.

The street was like many others in the home counties. Semi-detached, two-storey houses, each with their small parcel of land planted with flowers and devoid of weeds. Some had been extended at the back, the side and up into the loft but all had once been the same, built from the same basic plan and offering identical accommodation within. Outside, parked on the street, a row of parked vehicles offered a single space large enough for Wise's car. He strolled along the street in the yellow glow of the sodium street lights. Lights behind curtained windows were the only evidence of life in the suburban dwellings. He saw no one and no one saw him.

A light rain felt good on the shrunken skin of his face. He stopped and looked up at the individual drops showering down through the light from a ~~lamp~~ street lamp~~post~~. The drops were cold and the antithesis of the drops that had eaten away his skin. Water was magic, it washed away the dirt and grime, the blood from the streets and sustained all life. Without water there was nothing and yet too much would take life just as easily and painfully as the acid he had suffered.

He had once been fit. Wise had been an amateur middle-distance runner during his youth. He had kept up the training regime after joining the job, but it had become increasingly difficult to put in the training as he rose through the ranks. The hours in work had become longer and the leisure time eroded. He broke into a jog, it felt good. He remembered the times he had run in the rain – his favourite time. The jog became a run, the endorphins had kicked in as he ate up the tarmac. He stopped at the feeder road to the lab. He was out of breath, but it felt good. Perhaps the night offered him the opportunity to get his stamina back? No one would look at him twice; joggers ran at all times of the day and night and he'd be just like the rest.

Wise walked slowly towards the main gate. He could see the guard hut illuminated by the light inside. Bob had told him there would be three guards working the night shift. One in the box and two taking it in turns to patrol the perimeter fence. There was no hurry, he'd have to watch for the guards and time the patrol. He had all night.

The feeder road was lined on each side by a low hedge, well maintained and cut into a square profile for its entire length. Wise dropped to his knees and crawled behind the hedge furthest from the guard box. It took him ten minutes to crawl to the end near the security barrier. The guard in the box could be seen through the open door. The man was big, dressed in the company uniform and reading a Kindle. A ten-foot-high chain-link fence surrounded the complex with a curl of razor wire affixed to the top. Twenty-foot poles were dug into the ground at fifty metre intervals with strong lights pointing down onto the ground outside the fence. Beyond the fence, the compound was dark; ideal for a nocturnal escapade.

Wise checked his watch and smiled. Two minutes to go. He was in position and now all he needed was for Bob to keep to his end of the bargain. Bob had agreed to create a diversion. All the guard wanted in return was for his involvement to be kept out of any subsequent proceedings. Bob was a good man. He still thought like a copper and Wise would do whatever he could to keep him in the clear.

On the stroke of 10:30, as agreed, the alarm at the rear of the building began sounding. Wise watched the sentry set aside his Kindle and step out of the box. He heard him speak into his radio but couldn't quite make out what was being said. He guessed the guard was on high alert, probably intending to follow a set routine devised by some paper-pusher to ensure all guards complied with some health and safety directive. Wise also knew there'd be an element of panic setting in too. It didn't matter how well people trained for incidents, when the shit really hit the fan some of that cool-headed training went out the window.

He heard a door open at the side of the main building and watched as a dozen white-coated employees filed out into a car park. That was his signal to move but the sentry hadn't done what Bob said he would do. The sentry was to open the main barrier for emergency vehicles and make a call to the security command to update them. Why wasn't he making the call and why hadn't the barrier opened? ~~Perhaps the~~had the fool ~~had~~ forgotten the basics of his training?

Then the sentry seemed to remember his role and hit a button inside a waterproofed aluminium column and the barrier opened quickly. Then, as Bob suggested, the guard walked into the box and made a call.

Running for the opening gate, Wise slipped past the security box as the guard spoke animatedly into the handset. The lights inside the perimeter began to switch on, one after another, a chain reaction to the possible emergency situation that had activated the alarm. Wise knew it was a false activation, Bob said he would do something to set it off, he hadn't told Wise what it would be, but it clearly had worked.

Wise reached the corner of the building and checked the white coats milling under a light. Some smoked whilst others seemed impatient. Wise backed away and headed for the main entrance. The reception was unattended, the sole night guard had probably gone to check on the source of the disturbance. Wise pulled the security pass he had taken from the doctor – fully expecting it to be deactivated after the loss had been discovered. Thankfully, Bob had reactivated it – as promised – and the door hissed open on automatic hinges. He stepped through and headed up a flight of marble steps to the first floor. Here, Bob had told him, would be Levison's office.

The floor was a maze of corridors. Coloured tape lines on the floor reminded him of a hospital, each colour would lead to a department, but Wise had no idea which department Levison's office would be found in. He took a chance and crept along the nearest passageway. Signs for Petro-Chemical Research made him stop and retrace his steps. Another corridor led to the Department for Genetic Research and he guessed that sounded more hopeful. He walked quickly as the alarm suddenly stopped. The workers would be returning to their stations soon.

The last door on his left bore the name plate he was looking for. 'Dr L Levison. Director of Operations.' Wise donned a pair of rubber gloves and put his good ear against the blonde coloured hardwood and listened. There was no sound other than the voices he could hear in the corridor below and the moans of the white coats as they took the staircase to the floor he was on. Wise tried the handle, but it was locked. He used the pass card but that did nothing. There was nothing for it, he had to move fast. He stepped back and kicked out – hard – just below the lock. The door cracked and the lock gave way. The door flew open and Wise donned a pair of rubber gloves and grabbed at the handle before it slammed against the wall. He stepped inside and closed the door behind him. Thankfully, there was little mess from the forced entry and what little evidence ~~of it~~there was, had been ~~was~~ quickly collected and dropped in the waste bin next to the impressive walnut desk. The desk was clear of all but a Mac computer and a single black ballpoint pen. The tabletop had been polished to a high sheen and the shelves of books that occupied two walls were equally neat and tidy. Levison looked like he was a man after Wise's heart. A Xerox copier occupied the far corner and looked well used, clearly not a machine Levison believed was part of his cleaning remit. A neat, grey row of metal filing cabinets looked out of place amongst all the polished wood. Each cabinet held four deep drawers, and each had a single lock. Each drawer, in turn, had a cardboard label set in a holder, and each had neatly typed words.

    Wise scanned the labels and stopped at one that stood out from the rest. It was the only one labelled as a project. 'Project Future's Past' seemed an odd name; odd enough to attract Wise's attention. He forced the end of a small pocketknife he had always carried as a detective into the narrow gap between the top drawer and the frame and forcibly bent the metal until the lock gave way. Ignoring the other drawers, he opened the one that mattered and flicked through the files inside. Each was named and all looked innocuous apart from the names; they seemed odd, like an A-Z of the great and the good from the science history books. Curie, Darwin, Edison, Faraday, Tesla, Pasteur, Newton, Galileo, Einstein, Hubble, Hawking. None were adhering to alphabetical order or, if they had been, someone had disturbed that order and, going by the order within Levison's office, Wise couldn't imagine the man being any less orderly with his filing.

Intrigued, Wise pulled the file named Hawking from the drawer and placed it on the desk. He switched on his phone torch app and began to read. A series of six photos seemed to show the growth of a boy into a man; from about twelve months old to what Wise guessed was early thirties. No personal details were recorded other than something that looked like a library reference search number. A sheet of what looked like a coded printout was attached with a number of the lines ringed in red ink. What the hell? The boy-to-man was certainly not Hawking and he doubted the great, late scientist had any idea that his name had been used in the coding of the research. The names were code, he was sure of that, and that meant they were hiding something. A sheet of numbers was attached to the file. He checked another file and the sheet was attached to that too. One of the string of numbers was circled in red in the file code-named Hawking. A different string of numbers was circled in the second file. He had no idea of what the code meant but he knew, somewhere deep in his soul that it was important. He hurriedly took several sheets of the code from the file and ran them through the photocopier. Another file showed similar images but this time of a red-haired girl who had grown into an attractive woman. The voices were getting louder, the machine whirred and flashed, and every sound seemed somehow louder than they should be. The last sheet was spat from the copier and Wise folded them and tucked them inside his coat pocket just as he heard two voices outside the office door. They had noticed the damage and one began to shout for security.

***

Big Mike walked along the corridor towards the two men in the obligatory white coats. They were typical university wimps, wouldn't know how to fight their way out of a paper bag. He hated them. They thought they were better than him because they had certificates to say so. Big Mike snarled at them as he reached the office door. He had a degree from the university of fucking hard knocks and he wouldn't have called for help if he'd seen his office door kicked in. Levison stood next to a junior researcher. They could have been brothers, both tall and thin, balding and had complexions that reminded him of Captain Black the Mysteron convert. Without a pause, Big Mike pushed the men aside and shoved the door open. The door clattered against the wall as he stepped inside and switched on the light. A filing cabinet drawer was open and the lid on the photocopier was scattered with sheets of paper. There was no point in searching the office for the intruder – there was nowhere to hide – the open window behind the desk was all he needed to know that the burglar had gone.

## CHAPTER 7

It was a flat-out run and not a jog this time. Wise raced back along the road towards his car. The sentry had given chase as soon as he saw him run out through the barrier, but he had soon given up. He was no match for Wise's pace. All those years of training had not gone to waste, even if he was now about to collapse from exhaustion. His ankle throbbed from the shock of landing on the lawn beneath Levison's office window but the slope down from the building towards the car park had helped him roll and reduce the risk of injury.

The drive home gave him time to think.

Monroe was waiting as Wise parked his car outside his flat.

"What the hell have you done?"

"Follow me up to my flat and perhaps you can make sense of what I've got?" Wise said.

Monroe filled the kettle and dropped two tea bags into spotless mugs. "Please don't tell me you've done something you shouldn't?"

"Ask me no questions..." Wise grinned. He produced the sheets of code and smoothed out the creases on the dining table. "Take a look at these."

Monroe poured hot water into the mugs and added a dash of milk for them both. He carried the mugs to the table.

Wise grabbed two slate coasters and slipped them under the mugs.

"What is this?"

Taking a sip of tea, Wise shrugged. "Acquired these earlier from a friend."

It was clear Monroe didn't believe him but seemed content to let things ride. "Oh yeah?"

"Looks like a load of mumbo jumbo but I've seen something like it before."

Monroe nodded as he examined the sheets. He pointed to a line of tiny text in the upper margin of each sheet. "What the hell is 'Project Future's Past?'"

"Can you get someone in the Home Office lab to take a look? I think this shit is D.N.A. code. That in itself is not unexpected, hell, the place is a genetics lab, but it's the strange inferences with these dead characters and the photos of kids through their development that disturbs me; what the hell are they doing looking at dead people?

"Of course. Yes, that's what it looks like."

"How long will it take to get the boffins to tell us what it all means?"

"I honestly don't know but I can get it to them first thing, as soon as they open for business today.

Can't guarantee they'll do anything with it though. If this is classified material, they'll want clarification of authority to look at it and that'll be a problem."

"What about any connections there you could ask... to call in a favour?"

Monroe nodded. "I'll try. There is someone I could ask but I don't want to drop her in the shit."

"Great. So, what do you want me to do next?"

"Anything that's not illegal would be nice."

Wise read the police file for the third time. Monroe had left him alone while he delivered the sheets of code to the lab. It was clear, without doubt, that a serial killer was on the loose in London.

He grabbed a well-worn street map of London and opened it on the table. Taking a red marker from a kitchen drawer, he began marking out the location of each murder. "Fuck," he said as he realised they were all within a three mile radius of Whitechapel, world famous, primarily, as the site of the nineteenth century infamous Jack the Ripper. Did this mean there was a copy-cat? Were there similarities? He logged onto his laptop and began to search on the long-dead killer. The Modus Operandi (MO) was the same, the victims had their throats cut, abdominal mutilations and the visual similarities in the victims look

~~victims.~~ ~~But there was one big is~~ Martine ~~with the connection; the Ripper murders occurred in 1888.~~

Wise taped the map to a bare area of wall that once displayed a large photograph of him and Daria. He had taken it down the day she left and it had remained in the cupboard under the stairs ever since. He reached for his pack of cigarettes; he thought better with a smoke but there was just one left. He stepped out onto the small balcony and lit the cigarette. He watched the traffic and the people below in the narrow mews road. People were going about their business without a glance in his direction. He could see into the apartment opposite and turned his gaze away as a young woman stepped up to the window, smiled briefly at him and then closed the blinds. The street was no wider than a single carriageway, barely wide enough for a medium sized van to pass along but it was always busy. The close proximity of the building opposite had been a reason Wise had considered rejecting the apartment when he moved in several years ago, but the rental had been too attractive to turn down. Now he rarely gave it a second thought, other than when the woman opposite occasionally appeared at the window in the nude. She was an exhibitionist and who was he to complain? He smiled at the thought as he inhaled the toxic smoke. He needed more cigarettes. He locked the balcony door and slipped on his leather jacket. The walk to the local corner shop took less than three minutes and he stocked up with two packs of the cheapest French cigarettes and bought a bottle of bleach and some blue dishcloths.

He took the stairs back to his apartment and stopped outside his door. The door jamb was damaged. Someone had forced his door. He'd been away from the apartment less than ten minutes. That meant someone was probably still inside. Wise grabbed his mobile phone from his coat pocket and sent a text to Monroe; 'My door has been forced. Think someone is inside. Going in.' He dropped his phone back into his coat pocket, zipped up his leather jacket and pushed the door open slowly. He stopped inside and held his breath; listening for any sound that would confirm the presence of intruders. Nothing.

He took another step then froze as he heard a floorboard creak. Whoever it was in there knew Wise was there too. It was a stand-off. Wise knew he could wait for Monroe to arrive with the troops but by that time it might be too late. He took a deep breath and walked through the open door into the kitchen where a small runt of a man was standing, grinning at him. He was no more than five feet tall and couldn't have weighed more than a jockey.

"What the he'...?" Wise said just as a heavy arm clamped around his neck and he was pulled back against the wall. Wise struggled but he couldn't breathe, the pressure on his windpipe was stopping the air from entering his lungs and the strength was draining from him. The blood flow through the carotid arteries was being cut off and he knew he had less than thirty seconds before he blacked out. He had to act fast. Wise stopped struggling and stamped down hard where he guessed his attacker's foot might be. It struck home, the heel of his shoe connecting with bone. He heard the man holding him grunt with pain as Wise followed through by dropping his right arm down and slamming his balled-up fist back into the man's groin. The pressure on his throat eased and Wise twisted free. Then all went black.

The thin man was grinning when Wise regained consciousness. He was holding a taser and even though Wise was still groggy it didn't take a genius to realise the little man had zapped him. "What the fuck?"

Wise was tied to one of his own kitchen chairs with cable ties.

"I have a message for you, Mr Wise."

"Couldn't you just text me or something?"

The thin man smiled. "Digital communications are overrated, I think, don't you?"

"Not really. They generally don't carry fifty-thousands volts."

"Actually, it's only xero-point-zero-zero-two-one amps, but it's the way they send the current into the muscles that I find fascinating," he laughed, "you should have seen your face. You looked like a fish with epilepsy."

"Very fucking funny, I'm sure. So, what's the message? Has mum invited us all out to dinner?"

"Unfortunately, nothing quite so pleasant. I have a message from someone who would very much like you to desist in your participation with Mr Monroe."

"Oh? And what participation would that be?"

"Don't play dumb, Mr Wise. Let's keep this simple. I told my employer that you would probably ignore any such warning so took it upon myself to make sure you do desist."

"And what would that be, exactly?"

The thin man pointed the taser at Wise and fired.

\*\*\*

The sound of gentle ticking was all that registered in Wise's mind as the vivid dream of a white rabbit carrying a pocket watch faded and his vision cleared. His head pounded as he turned it slowly to search for the sound of the clock. Less than three feet from his face was an improvised explosive device. Like something from a Road Runner cartoon film, the device looked ridiculous but what it threatened was anything but that. Coloured wires led from a battery box to the alarm clock and a slab of what looked like modelling clay, but Wise knew this modelling clay was not for playing with.

The digital clock readout was counting down. Forty-eight, forty-seven, forty-six.

"Shit!" Wise rolled over onto his side, then onto his knees, the chair restricting him as he forced himself over, face pressed into the wooden floor. He sat himself upright then shuffled over to the kitchen counter and, with all the force he could muster, drove the chair back into the unit. He felt a leg of the chair crack, but it held firm. He could no longer see the countdown but knew there was little time left. He slammed backwards again and this time the leg broke free. Wise slipped his hand free of the broken stump then grabbed a knife from the dishwasher and cut the remaining ties.

He glanced at the timer as he headed for the door. Twenty-one, twenty.

The door was locked. He looked for his keys but knew the thin man and his sidekick had probably taken them. "Shit, shit!"

The balcony.

He rushed to the balcony door, thankfully, the thugs had not thought to lock that too. Wise opened the door and stepped onto the balcony. There was nowhere to hide from what was about to happen. The block of flats opposite was a good fifteen feet away, not far in the grand scheme of things. The alley was wide enough for service vehicles but now played host to rubbish bins. He looked back at the timer, he could see it through the open door. Five, four, three. His apartment was on the third floor – too far to jump but what other chance did he have? He stepped up onto the balustrade and launched himself into the air, just as the I.E.D. exploded.

## CHAPTER 8

Big Mike had seethed as he confronted each member of the security team on duty at the time of the breach. A man was seen escaping from the window of an office on the first floor, as if that wasn't bad enough, the bastard had escaped from Dr Levison's office and that was trouble. Bob had denied any involvement in the break-in, he wasn't stupid. Big Mike wasn't a man to mess with. There hadn't been a single breach in security since Big Mike took control four years ago. He had been hired to ensure nothing leaked from the lab at a time when it was rumoured some serious research was leading to some sensitive outcomes. Bob had not been party to these outcomes, nor did he want to be. He was just happy to turn up for his shifts, get paid and go home. He was as sure as he could be that Big Mike didn't believe him. The big man had stood face-to-face, his stinking breath from a mouth full of rotting teeth so close to Bob's face that he almost retched.

"No one breaks my rule," Big Mike screamed at the security guards lined up against a wall in the man's office. Bob couldn't help ~~think~~thinking they were lined up to be shot. "If I find out the intruder had help from the inside then God help you," he continued. "No one fucks with me and this has just fucked with me." The veins in the side of Big Mike's bald head bulged and throbbed as his complexion turned a purple hue with rage. Bob hoped one of those veins would just pop and put the mad fucker out of business – permanently.

All eight guards said nothing other than to deny their involvement. They dared not speak, they had all heard of Big Mike's reputation for being a ruthless bastard.

Dismissed, Bob clocked off at the end of his shift and drove his old car from the lab and onto the main road in the direction of home. It had been a worrying night. He knew he had been right in confiding to Wise but that still didn't make him feel better. What if Big Mike found out it was him that had let Wise into the compound? It wouldn't take much for him to check the CCTV and see Bob talking with Wise at the main gate the day before the break-in. It also didn't take a genius for him to link the loss of the security card by the doctor who spoke to Wise that night and then the use of that card to break-in. It was only a matter of time before Big Mike worked it all out, and Bob knew he had to be careful. He needed a drink. The girls would be tucked up in bed and Julie would still be up, watching a film even if he was half an hour later than normal. The White Swan was less than a mile from his house and one pint wouldn't hurt.

He pulled into the car park at the rear of the pub and walked into the bar through the rear 'smokers' entrance. A cloud of smoke hung beneath the corrugated plastic roof of the smoker's shelter. A smoke was a good idea. He ordered a pint of the local brew and walked back out to the shelter. He lit a cigarette and sat on an oak bench under cover of the canopy. He saw the black motorcycle pull into the car park but paid it no attention.

\*\*\*

The motorcyclist switched off the engine and kicked down the stand. He kept the helmet on as he walked towards the smoking shelter. A man sat alone on a bench, sipping from a pint glass and puffing on a cigarette.

He pulled the blade from inside his leather jacket and held it concealed from prying eyes as he walked towards the pub. He stepped into the cover of the canopy and saw the man look up just as he thrust the blade into the man's throat. The look of shock and then horror on the man's face was satisfying. It would be the last time the bastard betrayed him.

***

The blood spouted from the wound as Bob collapsed onto the ground. The motorcyclist kept the visor down and walked back to the bike. The number plate was false and the leathers he wore were common to thousands of other motorcyclists in the country. There was no way anyone would link the killing to him.

Big Mike pressed the start button on the handlebar of the Suzuki, kicked the stand up and the gear pedal into first. The bike moved slowly out of the car park. No one would pay him any attention as he accelerated and headed home.

***

The photographs of Cindy Gray were draped with black ribbons. It was a tradition abandoned by the vast majority of people today, but Charlie Gray belonged to another era. He had not yet turned sixty but looked at least ten years older. There was no doubt that the events of the last week had aged him, but he had always looked older than his years. Dressed in a chocolate brown cardigan over a white shirt, his black tie was open at the collar. He stood at the back door, smoking a cigar and staring at the stars. Cindy was up there, somewhere. She had been his little bright star as a child and now she was the most brilliant celestial body in the night sky.

Cindy had grown into a headstrong young woman, but she had always showered Charlie with love. His wife, Martha had tried to warn Charlie that Cindy was heading off the rails, that she had been drinking too much and spending too much time in night clubs, but Charlie had dismissed her concerns as those of a caring but paranoid mother. Martha was always overprotective, and it was that enveloping love for her that had sent Cindy away a year before. It had not been an unpleasant split; Cindy had just told her parents that she wanted to find her own place to live, to have her independence. Charlie had been disappointed but understood. She was a young woman who needed space and her leaving would give him the opportunity to build bridges with Martha. They had drifted apart over the years, but he still loved her, and he knew she loved him too. It was just that Charlie had spent so many years working all hours that when he retired from the antique shop he couldn't rest. He had converted the garden shed into a workshop where he restored antique weapons – his specialism. He was so good at restoration that most of the major antiques dealers used his services whenever they were needed.

The Smith and Wesson revolver lay on the patio table. It was a fine example of a World War Two handgun, the type used by officers in the Great War and Charlie had restored it sympathetically. As a class one firearm, the gun should have been locked away in a safe, but he had been licensed to restore the weapons. He had always made them safe by removing the firing mechanism but, for some reason that now seemed to be fate, he had not done so with this one. A box of .38 rounds lay open alongside the gun.

Charlie's line of sight dropped from the stars to the table and the gun upon it. Martha had gone to stay with her sister in Morcombe for a few days. She had always run to her whenever they faced problems. She had never been able to confide in him. Now he was glad she had gone because that gun was his answer to this nightmare. He would soon be with Cindy. He stepped out of the back door and picked up the weapon. He shook six rounds out of the box and fed three of them into the cylinder. He had seen 'The Deer Hunter' and had wondered how anyone could play Russian Roulette and now here he was with the gun in his hand. Theoretically, it would be easy just to point the gun at his head and pull the trigger, perhaps stick it in his mouth. But that would be too easy. Fate had robbed him of his only child and fate had a lot to answer for.

He spun the cylinder and thrust the barrel into his mouth. He screamed as he pulled the trigger.

Charlie saw the stars, they were just like before, nothing had changed. Fate had determined that tonight would not be the night he would die. So, if he wasn't to die tonight then someone else would, perhaps not tonight but soon. The bastard that had killed his daughter would meet the same fate. He lit another cigar and suddenly felt a heavy weight lift off his shoulders, now he had purpose again.

## CHAPTER 9

"All units in vicinity of Spalding Street, Kennington, attend report of explosion from third floor flat. Units responding? M.P. over."

Monroe was travelling home when he heard the call come over the police radio. "Shit! That's where Wise lives," he said to no one.

"Detective Superintendent Monroe is responding," he shouted into the hands-free set.

"Roger, guv, other units are responding. Lima-three is enroute, along with Lima Delta-two."

"Roger that. I'm five minutes out."

Lima-four was the nearest L-Division area car, crewed by an advanced driver and a radio operator responsible for logging the calls and dealing with the incidents they attended in the Kennigton area. Lima Delta-two was the Brixton divisional van, used to carry additional troops to incidents and for conveying prisoners back to the local nick. It wasn't uncommon for neighbouring vans and response units to help out when the local vehicle was tied up and Kennington's van had already closed at a serious assault and wouldn't be able to attend.

"Fire service are now on scene and ambulance also enroute, M.P. over."

"Thank you, M.P. Be advised that this location is the home of retired D.C.I.~~C.I.~~ John Wise."

"Noted."

The thin man and his heavy accomplice sat in a dark colour Ford Transit and watched as Wise flew through the air, covering the fifteen-foot gap like an ugly and ungainly Superman, his arms and legs flailing as he tumbled towards the other building. They watched the smoke billowing out of Wise's apartment and saw Wise crash through the window of the apartment opposite and one floor below Wise's own. "Shit!" the thin man said. "We better make sure the bastard's dead. How the hell did he get to the balcony?"

"I told you to lock the sodding door."

Thin man glowered at the big guy next to him. "Remember your place."

The big guy sighed and nodded. He knew better than to anger his diminutive partner. What he lacked in size he made up for with a mean streak that would have put Hitler to shame.

***

Wise flew through the air, partly through his own power but mostly as a result of the blast. The wall of the opposite block of flats moved up through his vision as his trajectory began to arc downwards. Then he saw the window and hit it with full force. He smashed through the glass and the frame and landed hard on the landing of a stairwell.

Winded, Wise rolled onto his knees and gasped for breath. He felt blood running down his face and could see the cuts to his hands from the broken glass. He kept his head low, between his legs, and waited for his breathing to return to normal before slowly checking his arms and legs for breaks. Apart from the cuts, he knew he had escaped lightly.

The sound of approaching sirens was welcome. They'd search his block for casualties and probably wouldn't think of checking the block where he was. The sound of the thin man's voice was not as welcome.

Wise pulled himself to his feet. He could hear footsteps on the stairs just a single flight below. He guessed he must be on the second floor. Made sense. He was falling for most of the impromptu flight. There was a flight of stairs ahead of him that led down and another to his left that led up. He had to move.

\*\*\*

The thin man and his heavy accomplice sat in a dark colour Ford Transit and had watched as Wise flew through the air, covering the fifteen-foot gap like an ugly and ungainly Superman, his arms and legs flailing as he tumbled towards the other building. They watched the smoke billowing out of Wise's apartment and saw Wise crash through the window of the apartment opposite and one floor below Wise's own. "Shit!" the thin man said. "We better make sure the bastard's dead. How the hell did he get to the balcony?"

"I told you to lock the sodding door."

Thin man glowered at the big guy next to him. "Remember your place."

The big guy sighed and nodded. He knew better than to anger his diminutive partner. What he lacked in size he made up for with a mean streak that would have put Hitler to shame.

~~Thin man and his sidekick~~They were not trying to be silent as they raced up the concrete stairs.

*\*\*\**

Wise stood and staggered to the handrail leading upwards. His legs hurt, his back felt like it was on fire and so did his arms and his head, but he knew he had get to get away. He was in no fit state to fight one, let alone two, opponents just now. Had he been fit, he was certain he'd handle both men at the same time. Wise had been brought up fighting – all styles – boxing, karate, judo, aikido, anything and everything. He had immersed himself in all kinds of fighting techniques as a young man, achieving a junior black belt at the age of eleven in all the martial arts. He had become obsessed with fighting after he had been picked on by the local bullies as a kid. Two of the local thugs, a couple of years older than Wise, had decided they would take his dinner money as he walked into school. Wise had put up a fight but had lost that encounter. He had sworn there and then that he would never lose another fight, and, to date, he hadn't. Since the acid burns, he had trained at home, behind closed doors, and missed the companionship of the dojo. He was also wary of the delicate nature of the skin grafts that he had been subjected to since that fateful day. The last thing he wanted was to have to return to hospital for remedial surgery to damage caused in a fight.

Feeling returned to his legs as he began to increase his pace up the stairs. Flight after flight he climbed. He reached the top of the stairwell and pushed through the emergency exit and out onto the roof. He couldn't help thinking about the similarity with Quasimodo as he looked around the flat roof. Fuck the bells, he thought as he ran towards the far end of the roof as the door behind him burst open and the thin man stepped through. Wise checked behind him and saw thin man raise his right hand into the air and take aim with what looked like a handgun.

"Shit!" Wise shouted. He had reached the edge of the roof and there was nowhere to go. The flat top roof edge gave way to a steep, inclined, tiled section that dropped some five metres before it ended at what looked like a vertical drop. Wise knew there was only two options. Option one was to try and dodge the gun fire and fight it out with two thugs or take his chance with the roof and hope for the best.

\*\*\*

Thin man had Wise in his sight, the iron sight was right in the middle of the mass and thin man knew how to shoot. He began to squeeze the trigger, smooth and firm, legs apart, balance right, left hand supporting the right, right arm locked out before him. Goodbye Wise. Even at twenty metres, thin man wouldn't miss his target. Then, the big thug burst through the roof door, straight into thin man as the trigger reached the release point and the nine-millimetre round cracked from the pistol.

Both thugs lost their balance, but crucially, thin man had missed his target.

\*\*\*

Wise took a chance. He slipped off the edge of the roof, eyes wide with terror, hands ready to catch the guttering at the bottom edge. He hoped it had been well maintained and wouldn't break off with the sudden weight applied to it.

It was more of a fall than a slide, the angle too steep to take much of the velocity out of his decent. Wise grasped at the gutter as he hurtled over the edge and screamed as he saw the ground far below and the Fire Engine parked in the courtyard, blue lights flashing, causing a strobe effect that seemed to slow down time. Wise caught the gutter but, as he feared, it didn't hold his weight. It slowed him considerably but the old fittings that had secured the guttering to the building for more than seventy years gave way and Wise began to fall again.

\*\*\*

The big thug rose from his knees and stared straight into the angry face of thin man. "You fool!" thin man screamed. "I had him and now he's gone."

"Now he's dead," the big guy grinned. "He's jumped. He won't survive that fall."

Thin man was tempted to kick his big colleague in the face just for the pleasure of seeing him bleed but thought better of it. He was right. There was no way Wise could have survived a six storey fall onto tarmacadam. Thin man wanted to go to the edge and to see the mangled remains of Wise far below but he knew the emergency services would be there and the first place they'd look when someone falls or jumps from a building is the place they fell or jumped from. It was too risky. "Come on. The cops will be coming up here soon. Let's go," he said.

***

Wise was winded for the second time in a matter of just minutes. He wondered if he'd done his lungs any serious damage as a result. His right hand hurt like hell where it hit the edge of the balcony. He couldn't believe his luck that the floors on that side of the building had balconies too. He had hit the first one down from the roof and twisted his ankle before he fell against the balustrading. A bruise appeared almost instantly on the edge and back of his hand, a red scrape at the centre of the rapidly blueing mass. He stood and limped back from the edge and leaned back against the balcony door. He couldn't hear voices above and hoped the thugs had believed he'd fallen to his death. He waited for a moment then turned to peer into the apartment through the glass door. There, staring back at him, was an elderly lady. Her expression was blank, neither confused nor worried, just blank. He wondered if a strange man falling onto her balcony was a regular occurrence. He doubted it very much. He smiled and waved his aching hand. The old lady matched his smile and waved back.

"Excuse me," he said loudly, "any chance of letting me in so I can leave through your front door?"

Now the woman looked confused.

"Er, I was fixing the guttering and slipped," he lied.

The woman nodded and seemed happy with his explanation. She clicked the lock and slid the door open.

"Thank you, so much," Wise said. "Thought I was a gonner then. Bloody landlord should have sorted the gutter out years ago,"

She nodded. "Aye, always pouring rain onto my balcony," she agreed.

It will now, Wise thought, as he looked back to the broken pieces of the guttering.

"Would you like a cup of tea?"

Wise grinned. Even though his entry was less than conventional, he guessed the old lady rarely got visitors to her apartment. "I'd love a cuppa."

Future's Past by David j Henson

## CHAPTER 10

"Any sign of John Wise?" Monroe asked the Chief Firefighter, a thirty-something woman dressed in full protective gear. Even in her kit she looked strangely appealing when she removed her white helmet with two parallel black stripes denoting her rank. Her blonde hair was cropped short and any style she preferred had been squashed out of shape by the sweaty headgear., S still, Monroe thought she must be an attractive woman and wondered how she had got herself into her position. He knew, from his own experience in the police, that equal opportunities policies had opened the door for women and at least a third of the top jobs in the police were now taken by women. Some had proved themselves worthy of the posts and others hadn't, but that was the same with his male colleagues. Some of the top male officers weren't worth their pay grade. Monroe had risen through the ranks from the ground up. He had done his time on the streets as a constable, shown his worth for a move to the CID and then, under the mentorship of John Wise, he'd found his calling within the Criminal Investigation Department. He owed Wise a lot and now he was standing outside his former colleague's apartment as the place burned.

"No sign of anyone in the apartment but that doesn't mean anything until we sift through it when things have gone cold," she said.

"How long will that take?"

"Who knows," she shrugged. "Probably won't get to that stage for the next twelve hours or so. Lot's to check for health and safety before we go poking around."

Monroe nodded. He'd been at several fires over the years and knew she was right. It was just so frustrating.

He watched the fire officer don her helmet and begin shouting orders to the team battling the inferno. Groups of residents were being ushered away from the scene by the uniform coppers. Monroe could only guess at their heartbreak at seeing their homes destroyed by the fire that now engulfed the whole building as a second fire tender arrived and instantly began unrolling the hoses and ladders.

\*\*\*

He was in no hurry. Wise thought it best to let the thugs think he had died in the fall from the roof. That would buy him a little time, at least.

The old lady said her name was Mildred Moloney. She was nearly eight-seven years of age and, as Wise had suspected, had no relatives to visit her. She said she had one friend, another old lady who lived on the ground floor of the block, but she hadn't been too well of late and Mildred had not seen anyone for nearly two weeks. Wise felt sorry for her. She had seen him wince when he tried to lift the China cup with his injured hand, and she disappeared into the kitchen for a moment and returned with a bowl of warm water and a bandage. She insisted that Wise let her dress the injury and he had to admit she had done a great job.

"I used to be a nurse," she explained as she made no attempt to hide her inspection of his facial burns. "That must have hurt like buggery," she said.

Wise nodded. "It did."

"Looks like acid?"

"How can you tell?"

"I can see the tracks of the stuff as it ran down your neck to your shoulder and chest."

"It was a bugger, alright," Wise said and then forced a smile.

"I'm sorry," she said.

Wise shrugged. "It was a long time ago now."

"How did it happen?"

He sat back in his chair and began to tell Mildred the full story, something he had not told anyone since that fateful day.

"I was working as a Detective Inspector when I got a report of a robbery at a local bank."

Mildred smiled. "So, you're not a handyman, then?"

Wise laughed. "How can you tell?"

"It's your eyes," she said. "There's something going on inside your head and it has nothing to do with fixing gutters."

He said nothing but continued back to the day three years ago. "Things got personal when I heard my sister and her husband, were inside."

"Wow. That must have been terrible."

"It was," Wise nodded and took a sip of his tea. "My sister had just started working at the bank. She was the owner of a cinema left to her by our parents. Times were hard and Peter, her husband stayed at the cinema whilst Martine got the job to supplement their income. She had never wanted to work there but, as I said, times were hard. Rob had dropped in at lunch time to take her out for something to eat and I often wonder why those little quirks of coincidence chose to conspire together at that time on that day," he looked at Mildred who nodded. "Anyway," he continued, "the officer in charge of the incident had done everything right. He'd sealed off the scene and had called in the armed response. I was working with the Flying Squad at the time on a bunch of armed robbers that had been making a nuisance of themselves across London and I had been driving to a stakeout, so I was armed. I arrived and wanted to get in there, before the guns started firing. I was ordered to stand my ground and not to interfere, but I couldn't do that. My sister and brother-in-law were inside. I felt helpless. Then I waited for the inspector at the scene to brief the armed response units and took the distraction as my opportunity to try something myself."

"What did you do?"

"I walked through the cordon and up to the bank door. I knocked and they let me in. I guess they thought an extra hostage; a copper, would be a bonus for them."

"No one stopped you?"

"As I said, the officer in charge was distracted and the uniforms at the scene knew me and thought I was acting under orders. I regret it now, not just because of the acid and the other things that happened in there but because I also dropped the senior officer in the shit. He was busted to sergeant and is still in the charge room of my local nick. It's fair to say he hates me. Can't say I blame him."

"So, what happened inside?"

"They had guns, four men, I saw three of them, one was no older than twenty and the other two were in their thirties, I guess. One of them stayed out of my sight. Then the armed response team moved in and all hell broke out. My brother-in-law started cutting up, trying to free himself. ~~I shot one as the robbers began shooting~~<u>As the robbers began shooting, I shot one of them</u>. ~~One~~ <u>Then another</u> ~~of them~~ put a bullet into my brother-in-law. I saw my sister's face; she just fell apart. I tried to go to her but then I felt it… the acid. The shit I hadn't seen<u>,</u> standing behind me, threw it in my face. He must have been carrying it just to cause serious injury."

Mildred shook her head and reached across the table. She let her hand rest gently on his. "I'm so sorry. What about you brother-in-law?"

"He died on the way to the hospital. Massive blood loss. But there's more. I was in agony and heard the gun fire as the armed police opened fire. An old lady was killed, and I was to blame. The inquiry said I should have stayed out and that my actions, whilst not the direct cause of the deaths, was a contributory factor. My bosses took it easy on me at the start. I was in hospital for so long I thought they'd forget about me. As soon as they could, they charged me with gross misconduct, but the Police Federation argued that I should have been praised for acting rather than be disciplined. In the end, I think the publicity began to turn in my favour when they saw the mess on my face and then I received a reprimand for disobeying an order."

"Did they sack you?"

"No. I resigned. There was so much bad feeling at the station, they all knew I was the catalyst for the mess there and I couldn't really do my job looking like this, now could I?"

"I think you look distinguished. We all bear the scars of our lives, some have more than others and some scars are more obvious, but we've all got them... somewhere." The old lady smiled sweetly and squeezed Wise's hand.

Wise felt emotional. He had spent the last three years supressing the pain and anguish that threatened to destroy him. Now, here he was, telling all to someone he didn't know and nothing he could do now could stop the tears falling. Great sobs racked his body. He felt ashamed, not of crying but for not crying sooner. Mildred stood, she groaned as her legs took the strain, but it didn't stop her rounding the table and hugging Wise.

***

He checked his watch. He'd been in Mildred's flat for nearly two hours. She had listened to him as he had poured his heart out and then thanked him –

thanked *him*. Wise had hugged her as he left her apartment and promised to call in to see her again in a day or two. She had told him not to promise something he couldn't guarantee but Wise had sworn to her that it was something he wanted to do. Mildred had somehow eased the pain, both physical and mental and, whilst he knew he had a long way to go, a flicker of a light had begun to appear at the end of the long tunnel he had stared down for so long.

Wise nodded to a young man leaving the apartment next door to Mildred.

"Have you seen the fire, mate?" the lad said.

Wise nodded. "Must be a gas main."

The young man ran off down the stairs.

Wise checked the stairwell. He didn't think the thugs would have stayed around with the police swarming all over the estate, but he couldn't afford to take a chance. The lift was out of action – deactivated by the warden of the block during the fire in the nearby flats as a precaution. Made sense. The fire crews were still damping down the blaze and Wise stood in the doorway of Mildred's apartment block, out of sight of the emergency personnel who were too busy to look his way. He could see the silhouette of Monroe staring up at the mess that had once been Wise's apartment. The window had blown out and flames were still licking at the plastic frame. There'd be nothing to recover. Wise thought about walking up to Monroe but thought better of it. The thin man and his partner in crime might well be lurking in the shadows somewhere, waiting for Wise to appear. They would probably know by now that he had not died in the fall and would be trying to work out what had happened.

He had lost his mobile phone in the flat. He needed a new one, something cheap he could use to call Monroe.

Wise left the estate through the ground floor corridor of the apartment building and out through the door that led directly to the street. A twenty-four-hour convenience store occupied the corner of the street and he walked in the shadows, hoping the locals would be more interested in the conflagration than the scars on his face. He bought a burner phone – a cheap pay-as-you-go phone for under twenty quid and installed the sim. Monroe's number was easy to remember, he had called it enough over the years. He tapped out the number and waited.

## CHAPTER 11

'Number withheld.' Monroe considered ignoring the call but answered it on the fourth ring. He needed the distraction.

"Monroe?"

He recognised the voice. "John, is that you?"

"Who else do you know who sounds like me?"

He sighed. "Jesus, John. I thought you were dead. Fireman Sam is about to pick through your apartment for your remains."

"It's only a stroke of luck that my remains won't be found. Some bastards tied me to a chair and set off a bomb."

Monroe was stunned. "You what?"

"Someone wants me to stop poking my nose into the murders. Who do you think that might be, eh?"

\*\*\*

Thin man stood amongst the crowd of onlookers, pretending to be interested in the events unfolding at the apartment block but using the opportunity to study the block Wise had jumped from. Each floor had a balcony and Wise must have dropped off the roof onto the top one. There could be no other answer to his miraculous disappearance. He nodded to his big colleague and pointed to the block. They walked from the crowd and headed back to the building.

\*\*\*

"Where are you?"

"On the corner of the street, outside the convenience store," Wise said."

"Meet me at the entrance to the estate."

Wise ended the call and walked back in the direction he had come.

Monroe was waiting for him as promised. He waved to Wise then turned back towards the fire crews. They were shouting and pointing to the block of apartments opposite the blaze. One of the crews was hauling a hose and heading towards it.

Wise stopped. "What the hell?" He ran towards Monroe and the two men hurried back into the courtyard. Wise looked up. "Oh no." Mildred's apartment was on fire. The balcony door had burst open and flames were clawing at the brickwork. He began to head for the block, but Monroe grabbed his arm.

"The fire crew will sort it. Must have jumped the gap…"

Future's Past by David j Henson

Wise shook his head. "No. They've killed her."

## CHAPTER 12

He lit a cigarette and puffed the smoke out of the small crack he had left in Monroe's car window. Monroe had not objected to him smoking even though he hated the habit.

Monroe was now risking his career. The Met radio operator had just announced the description of a suspect leaving the scene of a suspicious death at the apartment building and anyone and everyone who knew Wise would know it was him. A witness had seen him leave the apartment just minutes before the apartment was torched.

"I didn't do it," Wise insisted.

"I know. We should go to the nick and explain."

"No. You know we can't. We can't let the bastards get away with this. This is somehow connected to the laboratory."

"There'll be a country-wide search for you. You know how it works."

"They won't believe me. They'll throw away the key. I can't just sit in a cell while this bastard is out there killing innocent people."

Monroe knew Wise was right. There was a lot of bad feeling in the local station and he wouldn't get any help there. "You'll have to keep your head down until this blows over."

"That might be a problem. You may have noticed I have nowhere to live."

"I can't put you up. If I got done for aiding and abetting a fugitive, I'd lose my job and pension and probably do some time, too."

Wise nodded. "I know, I wouldn't expect you to. But I don't think you'll need to." Wise pointed to a large red brick building at the junction of the road ahead. A faded sign bore the name of a ~~national cinema chain~~ cinema Wise knew well. "Pull over there."

"Do you think it's wise?... excuse the pun," Monroe said with a smile, but he felt anything but happy.

"I've got to face her again sometime. Now seems as good a time as any."

"What if she just rings the police and tells them you're there?"

"I'm running out of options. If she shops me, I'll just have to think of something else."

The car stopped in a line of stationary traffic at the junction and Wise opened the door. "Thanks, I mean it. I really appreciate your help."

Monroe shrugged. "Not like I have much of an option."

"You always have an option. We all have options. I took the wrong one three years ago."

He stepped from the car, closed the door and walked towards the cinema.

## CHAPTER 13

Godfrey Button was not a happy man as he walked away from the burning buildings. Doug had done it again. Godfrey had told him to just scare the old woman, but the big fool punched her so hard that she died instantly. All Godfrey wanted was for the woman to confirm that Wise had been at her flat, but she refused to say anything.

He had had no choice other than to hide the evidence by burning the place with her body in it. Two fires in one day was pushing things, even by his standards.

Brought up in a care home, Godfrey had been the runt of the litter. Smaller than everyone else his age, he had learned to fight from an early age and, ~~where~~ what he lacked in stature, he made up for it with a ruthless, mean streak. He would do anything and everything to win a fight and Doug had learned that the first time they had met.

Godfrey was sixteen when their paths first crossed. Mr McDonald; the manager at the home, had arranged a trip to Snowdon in Wales, to a camp for kids like himself. Doug had been there, waiting for the minibus to arrive and soon began pushing his weight around. There was only three days difference in age between Doug and Godfrey; Godfrey being the eldest.

Doug was the only black kid at the centre and at least a foot taller and three stone heavier, he looked like he had seen a lot of trouble in his formative years. His nose had already been broken and a thin scar ran from his left ear to his mouth. He looked tough, but he had made a big mistake picking on Godfrey. He had spat at the small lad and pushed him in front of Mr McDonald. McDonald had said nothing but watched as Godfrey walked away. Godfrey was convinced that McDonald had looked disappointed, as if he had expected Godfrey to fight back, but Godfrey wasn't going to get himself into trouble. He had experience of McDonald's anger and there would be time to get his revenge on the big lad.

The opportunity arose after dinner. The centre staff had welcomed the new kids and outlined the events for the following day. As the children were allocated their dorms, Godfrey had hidden a plastic, disposable knife in the sleeve of his hoodie. He watched Doug grin as Godfrey's name was added to the dorm that Doug was staying in.

Godfrey broke the rounded end of the knife and replaced it up his sleeve. The new sharp end dug into the flesh of his arm as he marched out of the dining hall towards the wooden building that would serve as the dormitory.

The kids filed into the big room, a rectangular space big enough for a dozen single bunks, six on each side with a small bedside table next to each for personal belongings and a wardrobe behind each for their clothes.

Godfrey picked an empty bed and lay down. He watched Doug walk towards him.

"Hey, fuck off, that's my bed," Doug snarled.

"I didn't see you lying here," Godfrey said.

Doug stepped towards him and, as he grabbed him by the scruff of the neck, Godfrey slid the knife from his sleeve and stabbed Doug in the face. The big lad didn't scream. He stood there and grinned. Godfrey was impressed and rather than the two lads becoming enemies they had strangely struck up a bond that had lasted ever since.

McDonald had grinned when the nurse had dressed Doug's wound and had called both boys into his room. He had made the boys shake hands and sent them on their way. Godfrey suspected the whole thing had been set up and it wasn't until several years later that it had all made sense.

## CHAPTER 14

Wise pressed the security buzzer set into the wall at the side of the large, Art Nouveau doors and waited. A small camera set in the unit whirred and turned to face him; then he heard a click as the door locking mechanism released. He pushed through the heavy door and reset the lock manually from inside. He heard the door to the box office open and then saw his sister staring at him.

After the incident at the bank three years ago, Martine had handed in her resignation and returned to the cinema. She now ran the place pretty much on her own, with just a couple of part-time helpers during the screenings. The cinema had not been busy since the seventies, but it was in her blood and Wise could never imagine her leaving.

"What the hell do you want?" she snapped.

"Thought I'd catch a movie," Wise said awkwardly. He had not spoken to his sister since the court case and the Coroner's Inquest into her husband's murder, a death she had unfairly attributed to Wise.

Martine stared at him, a severe conflicted expression of anger with the slightest indication of relief at seeing him. Wise thought she had probably assumed he had succumbed to his depression and taken his own life. God only knew that he had seriously considered it many times, but he had never had the courage to follow it through. He had never felt ashamed of those feelings. They had made perfect sense to him at that time. His life had ended on that day in the bank and there was no point in continuing. The problem was that he still had a little voice in his head telling him that something might happen that would change his life for the better and, even though that was unlikely, he wanted to stick it out a little longer to see if that voice was telling him the truth. No miracle had happened and each day that voice began to fade until he stepped onto the edge once more. Then the little hopeful bastard in his head would start up again.

"I told you never to speak to me again," Martine snapped as she folded her arms defensively.

"It's been a long time…"

"Not long enough," she scoffed.

Wise stepped forward slowly and Martine stepped back towards the door she had entered through. Wise stopped. "I know I look like a monster, but I would never hurt you."

"You hurt me when you killed Peter."

Wise shook his head and sighed. He had heard this before, and he had no idea how to get it through to his sister that his actions were driven to save her and Peter that day. Nothing he said seemed to make a difference.

"I think you should leave now," she said.

"I don't have anywhere to go. There was a fire at my apartment. I've got nothing left."

Martine was incredulous. "So, you came here hoping I would help you out?"

"Someone is trying to kill me, Martine. A serial killer responsible for at least three murders, or one of the people involved with him, and I need to lie low for a while."

Now Martine was angry. "You came here knowing you'd put me in danger too?"

Wise held up his hands in surrender. "I just had no other option, I'm sorry. It was stupid." He turned to leave.

"I don't fucking believe you. You might have already put me in danger by coming here."

He stopped and turned. "No one knows I'm here. I checked that I wasn't followed. Only Monroe..."

"So, someone *does* know!"

He shrugged. "Monroe's a copper."

"I know who he is."

"He won't say anything to anyone. He can't afford to..."

"What do you mean by that?"

Wise sighed. He knew that if he was to get Martine to help him, he'd have to tell her everything. "An old lady was murdered too, after I had been talking to her, and now the police think it was me."

"You're a suspect?"

"Seems so."

"Then I should call the cops."

He nodded, resigned. "Might as well. I've got nowhere else I can go. It won't take them long to track me down. I'm not exactly able to blend into the crowd."

Martine stood defiant but her expression had softened.

"Nice to see you kept the old place open," Wise said as he looked at a poster for the film currently on show. "What time are you opening?"

"First showing is Downton Abbey at two and then I have Angel Has Fallen at seven-thirty."

He checked his watch. "Perhaps I'll watch the first showing. The cops can pick me up after the film if you hold off. I could do with a little distraction."

"Didn't think Downton Abbey was quite your scene."

"Heard good reports."

Martine nodded. "Thought you were a Marvel man?"

"Still am. I have more in common with those characters now, I suppose. Me and the misfits."

Martine said nothing for a moment, an awkward silence that seemed to search her soul. He could almost see the conflicting emotions run through her head. Finally, she let her arms drop and she turned to leave. "If you want to watch the film, you can help me clear the shit off the floor of the cinema before the customers start coming in. Should be busy. The film's been popular. More films like that we need."

Wise walked to a door at the side of the box office and heard the security lock buzz. He pushed through to the office behind. Martine was brandishing a vacuum cleaner with a long hose attached.

"You can start with this."

***

Doctor Lindon Levison had locked his office door and sat staring at the monitor. Things were not right. Everyone had changed, they had all clammed up. No one was talking about anything anymore. He read the memo and sighed. It was clear that someone at the top had a reason to throw a blanket over the operation. There was no need. He had it all under control. He was in charge and he had no intention of letting anyone else muscle in on his work. He was responsible for some of the greatest medical advancements of recent history and yet no one knew. That didn't bother him. He was a doctor and had never been interested in fame – fortune perhaps - but not fame.

He looked up from the screen as he heard the knock at his door. He could see the outline of Big Mike. It couldn't be anyone else with that outline. Another, smaller figure stood to his side and was gesticulating at the big man. He could hear Angie's raised voice, telling Mike that Doctor Levison wasn't to be disturbed but he knew Mike wouldn't let that bother him.

Angie meant well. She was new, a replacement P.A. for him that he had badly needed. Carole had left three weeks ago, just before that unfortunate death in the car park, and it had taken too long to find a replacement. Indeed, only Angie had applied for the post. Thankfully, she had been well qualified and more than able to do the job.

Levison rose from the chair and walked over to the door. He turned the lock and stood aside as he threw open the door. "Yes?" he said.

"We need to talk, Doc," Mike said.

Levison looked at Angie. She mouthed an apology and Levison nodded. "It's ~~okay~~OK, Angie. I need to speak with Mike. Give us five minutes and then we'll get down to the grant proposal."

"Yes, doctor," Angie turned on her heel and walked back to her desk in an alcove off the corridor opposite Levison's door.

Levison watched Mike walk to the desk and sit in his chair. He closed the door and growled at the big man. "I know you think you're some big-shot thug, but I'd advise you to move your arse out of my chair, if you still want to be working here this time tomorrow."

Mike grinned then stood. He stepped aside with a theatrical flourish and pointed to the chair. "All yours, sir," he said.

Levison walked past him and took his seat.

"I'm afraid that we have a bit of a problem," Mike said as he sat on the corner of Levison's desk.

\*\*\*

The glass pane in the office door was a problem but Angie wasn't too worried. She could listen in without putting her ear to the door. She pressed a button on the intercom she used to communicate with her boss. When it was installed it would have buzzed when pressed but the buzzer hadn't worked since she had worked there. She had discovered the anomaly on the first day and it had already come in handy. Good PAs needed to keep on top of things and there was no better way than listening in on conversations.

She caught the sound of Mike's voice. "...he has a sister. She runs a cinema near ~~in~~ Whitechapel. He'll be hiding out somewhere and I'm sure he'll be there. You want me to sort it or should I update the Muppets?"

"Tell the Muppets. And tell them not to fuck up this time."

## CHAPTER 15

As the opening credits for the movie began to play for Wise, two miles away, Godfrey Button and Doug sat opposite Isaac in a McDonald's restaurant.

Doug was wolfing down three cheeseburgers and large fries and had already finished one of the large Tango Orange drinks. Godfrey picked at a small portion of fries as Isaac sat watching them. He sipped from a steaming cardboard cup of coffee and smiled at the two men from a table several metres away. He wanted to turn away in disgust but needed them more than they needed him.

Isaac waited for Godfrey to finish his fries before he stood and walked to their table and sat alongside Doug. He spoke. "Where is he now?"

Godfrey and Doug had never met Isaac. They had been told to meet him at the restaurant but had no idea what he would look like. Godfrey was surprised; Isaac was nothing like he thought he would be. Both Godfrey and Doug had been told the contact was a man to be respected and to be feared. This guy looked more like a male model than a psycho. Godfrey shrugged his shoulders and picked at a fragment of fries stuck between his teeth.

The smile slipped from Isaac's face. "I was told you'd sort it. I can't have the bastard getting in the way, you understand me?"

"Of course, I understand you. I'm not fucking thick," Godfrey snapped back.

Isaac had to be careful, had to watch his words. "Of course not. I wasn't suggesting you were."

"Good," Doug said.

Isaac ignored the big man. Godfrey may not be stupid by Doug was as thick as two short planks and twice as dense. Isaac didn't like blacks and Doug wasn't just black, his skin was as black as coal. "Have you any idea where he's gone?"

Godfrey stared at Isaac for a moment, evaluating the smooth, good-looking man in the smart and expensive clothes. "So, you're the fucking crazy they told us about?"

Sitting back in his chair, Isaac folded his arms defensively and faked a hurt expression. "Crazy? Me? Surely not? Dedicated, astronomically intelligent, stunningly good-looking, and driven, would be descriptors I would prefer. Crazy suggests I'm not in control of my actions and I can assure you nothing could be further from the truth."

Doug snorted and attracted a piercing laser stare from Isaac.

"If you're so clever then why can't you sort out Wise?" Godfrey said, breaking the stare.

Isaac leaned forward and sipped his coffee. "It's not my decision. I'd be happy to sort him, but I've been warned off."

"Warned off? By whom?"

"Whom?" Isaac sniggered. "Been reading Janet and John, have you?"

Godfrey didn't understand. "Who the fuck is Janet and John? They got anything to do with the project?"

"There you go, you had to go and spoil the illusion of intelligence, didn't you?"

The thin man stood quickly and leaned across the table. Other diners looked his way, expecting action. "Watch your mouth, you flashy twat."

Isaac didn't flinch. His eyes rose slowly from his coffee and met Godfrey's. "Sit down. I won't tell you again," he said calmly. "You're drawing attention and that's not good."

Godfrey looked around and raised his middle finger to the nearest couple engrossed in the action. "What you fucking looking at?"

"Sit down," Isaac snapped.

He knew Isaac was right. Attention was never a good thing. They were three totally different looking men, as far removed from each other as it was possible to be and that meant they would be easy to describe if things got out of hand. They had to stay under the radar for now, but Isaac would be sorry for taking the piss out of him. Godfrey sat and snarled at the nearby couple as they stood to leave; meals unfinished and abandoned in fear.

"Who's warned you off?" Godfrey asked once more, this time a whisper.

"No names, you know the rules," Isaac smirked.

Godfrey thought for a moment then nodded. "OK. Well tell this... person who shall remain unnamed, that it's all in hand. We've got it covered, alright?"

Isaac stared at Godfrey then at Doug. "Make sure you do." He sipped his coffee again then set the empty cup on the table.

"What the hell have you done to get all these bigwigs foaming at the mouth?" Godfrey asked.

Isaac said nothing. His lips pouted as if he was a child scalded for stealing apples.

"It must be big," Godfrey continued. "Never heard so much panic before."

Now Isaac grinned. "I think they don't like me. I suppose I'm not exactly what they were expecting. They wanted someone who would be a good little robot, someone who'd toe the line and be a good little boy but that was never going to be. You can't create chaos and hope to control it."

Godfrey had no idea what the man was talking about and shrugged his shoulders.

"May I make a suggestion?" Isaac continued.

"About what?"

"Seems to me this Wise guy," he smiled, "excuse the pun, doesn't have many places he can hide. You destroyed his home, got him in the frame for the murder of an old woman and even his old mates in the cops are out to get him. That, I would suggest, limits his options."

Godfrey nodded.

"So, I'd start by looking into his background, his family and all that kind of shit."

Nodding again, Godfrey knew Isaac was making sense. "I was just about to do that," he lied to save face. Truth was, he hadn't really given Wise much thought. How many places could a disfigured man hide in without coming to the attention of the cops?

"Now, I'd suggest we need to find him before the cops do, and finish him before he blabs and starts pointing the finger back at you and me."

"Makes sense."

"I'm glad you think so because I've already done some checks on the man. Did you know he has a sister?"

Godfrey cringed. He knew he should have done the background checks but didn't expect Wise to be so slippery.

"His sister, Martine is the owner or manager of an ~~Odeon~~ cinema near~~in~~ Whitechapel. Shouldn't take much to find her and, by association it shouldn't be hard to find Wise either."

"~~The flea pit in Whitechapel? Not the Odeon anymore.~~ Private, small time set up, it is~~,~~." Godfrey enlightened him.

"Do you like the flicks?"

"Aye, now an' again," Godfrey said.

"I love the pictures," Doug said excitedly.

"Some good films out at the minute. Why not take the afternoon off and go watch one, eh?"

Godfrey began to laugh and nodded his head. "Yeah, why not?"

## CHAPTER 16

Downton Abbey was certainly not John Wise's type of movie. He had sat through nearly an hour before he realised that he had no idea what the film was about. His eyes were following the action, but his brain wasn't processing the images and the sound. He felt the tears running down his face and wiped them away, not from shame, no one could see him in the corner at the back of the theatre, he wiped them away because they didn't belong there. He felt angry, the tears were betraying him, they had no right to be there, no right at all. He punched the back of the chair in front of him. The theatre was over half full, but the other filmgoers had avoided sitting anywhere near the man with the messed-up face. The loud crack of his fist hitting the back of the chair was lost in the orchestral strains of the incidental music rising to a crescendo as the King made his appearance at the grand house on the big screen.

The pain in his knuckles was nothing compared to the pain in his head. It wasn't one of those pains that could be quenched by Asprin or Paracetemol. His pain was way beyond any kind of quenching. Some days it was manageable but other days it was unbearable. Today was one of those days where his head felt like it would explode. He knew the cause but that didn't make it any easier to deal with. He could feel the other monster, the one inside his head, taunting him, building the pressure like some cooker with a broken release valve, pulsing and building, pulsing and building and about to explode. He felt sick.

Wise stood and shuffled out of the theatre, using the alley chairs to guide him in the flickering light from the big screen. He reached the door and squinted as the bright light in the foyer added to the pain in his head.

He leaned against the wall as the door to the theatre closed silently on hydraulic hinges. The pain was getting too much to bear.

"You alright?"

He turned his head to see Martine standing beside him. He cracked a smile, not because he was alright but because he was pleased to see she looked concerned for him.

"I need to sleep."

Martine put her arm around him and led him towards a door marked 'Private.' "You go and get your head down upstairs."

The doorway led to a staircase to the first floor where Martine had her apartment. She and her husband had run the old Odeon cinema since her parents had died a decade before. It had once belonged to her grandfather in the days of silent movies. He had hit hard times in the early seventies and sold the cinema to the international movie theatre chain before they too decided they needed to rationalise during the birth of Netflix and Amazon prime. The family had maintained operational control of the business even during the ~~Odeon~~ days it had been owned by a national chain, but Martine's dad had bought it back more out of nostalgia than a hope of making it a going concern, but the purchase had coincided with the release of hundreds of good movies that had led to the business more than just holding its own.

The apartment was well furnished, better than Wise remembered it. "Fixed it up well," he said.

"I used the Criminal Compensation I had for the murder..."

"I'm sorry."

"So you keep saying. It wasn't much, the compensation. If he'd been injured in some ~~factory~~factory, he'd have had more but being killed in a botched robbery? It's a joke."

Wise sat in an armchair. "The courts pay more for a celebrity slandered than someone killed or injured in crime. It's a sick system."

Martine filled a kettle and flicked the switch to boil. "I'm having a cuppa. You want one?"

"Yeah… please."

She dropped tea bags into two mugs and then sat opposite her brother. "I called the cops."

Wise nodded. "I don't blame you."

"I called Monroe."

"Ah. What did he say?"

"Not much, just that he'd be grateful if I'd let you lie low for a while."

He nodded. "He's a good man. Not the twat I thought he had become."

"He thinks a lot of you."

"Yeah, well, he's in the minority." Wise smiled.

"What are you going to do?"

"I don't know."

"You don't know?" Martine said, incredulous. "You always know what you are going to do, always have. Even as a small boy you always had the answer to everything. Do you know how bloody annoying you used to be?"

Wise laughed. "I can guess."

Martine laughed too. "I know it sounds crazy, but I actually liked that about you. I could always rely on you to do what was needed."

"Until now?"

"Until that day when you decided to waltz into that bank and play the fucking hero."

He shook his head. "I wasn't being a hero. I was scared, Martine. For the first time in my life I was scared because I thought I was going to lose you."

Now she shook her head. "You scared? You've never been scared of anything. I've seen you in action, remember."

"I was scared that day, Martine."

She sighed and stood as the kettle boiled and began to rattle on its cradle. Martine poured hot water onto the bags and swirled them around with a spoon before sloshing milk on each. "Still taking two sugars?"

"Haven't taken sugar for years. Watching my figure."

"That's another thing about you. How did you get the fit and healthy genes and I got the fat ones?"

"You're not fat." Martine was far from being overweight but had always suffered insecurity with her body shape. "I used to train all hours."

"So did I."

Wise could feel his eyes closing. He was exhausted, battered and bruised. Martine handed him his tea and he sat upright to take a sip. "This is good. Not like the shit you used to make."

"It was Peter's favourite brew. Drank loads of it after he gave up the booze," Martine's voice cracked, and she began to sob.

Wise placed the tea on the carpet and leaned over to his sister. "I'm truly sorry, Martine. If I could go back in time and change things, I wouldn't change anything that happened to me, not the acid, nothing, but I would change what happened to Peter. The last thing I wanted was to ruin your life like that."

Martine leaned in towards her brother and hugged him. Then the sobs became wails of anguish. Wise let her cry. He wished he could do the same, but his tears seemed to have a life of their own. They never obeyed him, never betrayed his true feelings, just sneaked up on him when they weren't wanted.

A knock at the alleyway door broke the huddle.

## CHAPTER 18

The lab was a large complex of new and old technology. Hermetically sealed from the outside by a number of airlocks, the handful of technicians on duty were dressed in disposable white coveralls that extended to hoods and paper masks. Blue surgical gloves and loose disposable shoe covers completed the astronaut look.

One entire white wall was fitted with large flat screen monitors operated by the latest and most powerful computers to analyse the results of the tests being carried out by another group of similarly dressed technicians locked away in a separate part of the lab that housed the physical elements and materials for testing. Large windows to one side were covered in a light filter film that controlled the level of sunlight allowed to enter and could be controlled from a console to vary the amount as desired.

Levison was dressed like the others, no outward sign of superiority or rank evident. He walked behind the workstations and spent several minutes at each digesting the information provided for him on the screens.

He moved between the technicians, speaking only to clarify points of data from time to time. The information collected would be collated into a report for the secret government department and even more secret private financiers that were bankrolling the research.

Levison had been instrumental in the research from the outset and had been head of the laboratory during the forty years of the project. Now he was director of the entire complex, overseeing all the research at the lab. He had considered retiring but thought better of it. The two previous directors had not lived long after their retirements. One had died in a road accident just weeks after claiming his pension and jetting off to Spain. The Spanish police had recorded the accident as a result of drink driving but Levison knew Professor Appleyard had never drunk during the time he had known him. Of course, retirement might have changed all that. The second director had died of a heart attack at his home in Surrey. Doctor Marcel Coose had been a fanatical marathon runner before his heart attack. It wasn't exactly unheard of for a fit man to drop dead, but it wasn't something Levison had imagined would happen to Coose.

Professor Appleyard had proposed the project as part of his research into ageing and the fruits of that early work wereas synthesised into a genetic remedy to slow down the deterioration on a number of internal organs. Levison had been on board from the start but had no idea, until he became director himself, that the remedy had been recommended for use of only a select number of V.I.P.'s. The names of those given the magic bullet were never known to Levison but he suspected they were amongst the very top of UK society.

The deaths of the two previous directors worried Levison. He knew things that would cause a national scandal if they were ever leaked to the public. He had a number of safeguards in place, just in case the deaths had not been quite as they had been reported. Levison had created a website based around his hobby of fishing. He had uploaded a file containing a raft of incriminating data and information that clearly outlined the work that had been carried out at the lab in the name of H.M.G. That file required a password to keep it dormant at any time during a rolling seven-day calendar. It would automatically send itself to all major news outlets – papers, tv and radio stations – seven days later if that code was not entered. The site had been online for more than two years now and on at least three occasions Levison had nearly missed the deadline for the code input and released the incriminating emails to the unsuspecting world. He guessed that the work on the any ageing genes would not be that devastating for the company but the other work they had carried out since would certainly be earth shattering, especially now.

Returning to his office through the first of the airlocks, he stripped off his coveralls and dropped them through a 'dirty' hatch that took the items off to an incinerator before passing through the next airlock and out into the corridor. He walked past the canteen and took an escalator to the first floor. His office door was unlocked and that was against the protocols. He turned to Angie. "What's going on?"

Angie looked up from her computer. "I'm sorry, Doctor, but Mike made me let him in. He refused to say what he wanted in there but warned me I'd lose my job if I didn't allow him access. I'm sorry…"

Levison was clearly rattled by the disclosure but knew there was no point in shooting the messenger. He nodded his thanks to his PA and closed the door behind him. He leaned against the glass panel and Angie could see him clearly. He was worried.

What the hell was Mike after? Why was he in his office?

He began checking his desk and then his filing cabinet. Just one file had been removed and it was the one that would cause the biggest shit heap of a stir if it ever leaked. What the hell was Mike doing? He'd get them both in trouble.

Levison dialled Mike's mobile number and waited for several rings before the phone went to answerphone. He hung up ~~before~~ without leaving a message. Mike would recognise his number and know why he was calling. If everything was above board he'd call back, if not…

## CHAPTER 17

Godfrey and Doug stood outside the door marked 'Private' and waited for a response. They knew the woman was there because the girl serving popcorn had told them so. The girl had told them that Martine used a side entrance to her flat and that there was a door to the apartment from the foyer but that she never answered that door during performances. "Let's try the other door," Godfrey said.

They walked back along the alley and around to the front entrance to the cinema.

A handful of cinemagoers milled around in the foyer, loading up with sweets and snacks and soft drinks, waiting for the movie to end before they could take their turn to watch the next performance.

Doug watched them carefully, not wanting any of them to complicate matters by paying them any attention. A middle-aged couple stood together in a corner of the foyer, lost in an embrace. The man wore a trilby hat and a long overcoat, and the woman was dressed in a short leather jacket and black leggings.

The two men waited for a minute before Godfrey tried the handle to the apartment. The door opened and he nodded to the big man alongside him. "Come on. Looks like they weren't expecting our call," he whispered.

They climbed the stairs and reached a door at the top of the flight. The door wasn't locked, and Godfrey stepped aside for Doug to enter first. Doug pushed the door open into a hallway. Two doors led off to the left and two to the right. He walked along the passage and looked in through the first door to his left. It was partially open, and he could see it was a kitchen and living room combined.

He quickly checked the other rooms, two bedrooms and a bathroom. All empty. "There's no one home, Godfrey."

"Shit!" Godfrey pointed to the living room. Check the rooms, see if there's any clue where they could have gone. I'll do the bedrooms."

\*\*\*

Martine led the way to her car at the rear of the cinema. Her red Ford Fiesta was parked in a reserved bay. She clicked open the door and got behind the wheel as Wise walked around to the passenger seat. He waved at Monroe as his friend waved back and jogged off down the High Street.

Trish, a part-time help at the cinema, had called the flat intercom to warn them that she had had spoken to two thugs that wanted to know if a man with a scarred face was in the flat with Martine, and were now on their way to the side door.

They had just walked into the foyer when they saw the thugs enter. Wise had donned a trilby hat that had once belonged to Martine's husband Peter and had borrowed one of his long raincoats and thrown it over his leather jacket. Martine had snatched her coat from the hallway, and they had hurried down the other stairs into the foyer. Wise had pulled his sister into a hug and turned his face away from them. Martine had secretly watched them knock on the door to the apartment and then enter. That had been their cue to run.

Martine reversed her car out of the bay and out of the car park. She had no idea where they should go but anywhere was better than staying around. "So, nobody knew here you were?"

"Only Monroe," he said. Then he froze as he turned to look at Martine. She was clearly thinking the same thing.

***

It had been a while since he'd jogged last. Monroe ran along the High Street towards the bus stop. He had taken the bus rather than his car because he suspected someone was watching him. He was now convinced that someone at the laboratory was involved in the murders, especially after a report of the discovery of the body of one of the security guards last night. He hadn't had time to tell Wise, but he needed to know. He dialled Martine's phone. She had scribbled the number for him before they left her apartment. Wise answered.

"It seems one of the guards from the lab has been found murdered."

Wise felt a deep dread. "Not a guy called Bob, ex-job?"

"Don't know about the ex-job bit but his name was Bob."

"Shit!"

"I take it he helped you out?"

"Don't suppose it matters if I tell you now, does it? What happened to him?"

"Well, looks like he had gone for a drink after work and someone slashed his throat as he sat outside the pub having a smoke."

"Jesus. Any witnesses?"

"None that have come forward."

There was an awkward silence. Then Wise spoke. "How did the bastards know where to find me?"

Monroe didn't reply.

"I think you need to be straight with me."

Then it dawned on Monroe. Wise thought it was him who had told the thugs of his whereabouts. "You can't really be thinking I set you up, surely?" Wise said nothing. "Why would I do that? Think for fuck's sake. Why would I do that?"

"Truth is, I don't know anything anymore. Nothing is what it seems."

Monroe was furious. "If you think…" he shouted but was cut off before he could finish his rant.

"Of course I don't think you set me up," Wise shouted back. "I just don't know what the hell is going on."

Wise's words defused Monroe's fury. "OK. Just stay low for a while until I can sort this."

"Easier said than done."

"Don't tell me where you're going, don't tell anyone. Just keep the phone charged."

Wise knew anyone with the technology would be able to trace a phone. "I'll buy some burners and send you the numbers as and when. That OK with you?"

"Perfect. Just keep moving."

## CHAPTER 19

The file contained everything Mike already suspected. He grinned as he sipped from a hip flask of rum. He sat in his Range Rover. The blacked-out windows were total, no one could see in. The windows were illegal in the U.K., but that didn't matter to Mike. He had been stopped several times by police and warned and even reported for the offence, but no summons would ever find its way through his letterbox.

Mike had photocopied the contents of the file and stored the images on a thumb drive. He would have bet a small fortune on the fact that Levison had done the same. The shit was hitting the fan big time and Mike knew he would be just a piece of collateral damage when that shit began to pour down on everyone. He had to be prepared. Mike had always been the best prepared of anyone he ever knew. It had kept him alive when others had died. Two tours of Afghanistan and several trips into countries that didn't know he was there had helped to develop his extreme sense of caution. Taking the security job at the lab had been an easy option for him. He had left the S.A.S. under a cloud after a covert job in the Saudi capital had gone horribly wrong and almost resulted in an international incident. The blame for topping the wrong target had been laid firmly at Mike's feet but he had been prepared for that too and had escaped with a no option offer of the job at the lab from some Whitehall suit. The S.A.S. were happy to see him leave before they had to return him to his unit, and the government knob had laid down the ground rules. Mike was working for the suit, not the lab. It was his priority to keep a close eye on the day-to-day running of the complex and to report everything back to H.M.G. via the suit. The suit had said his name was Myers, but Mike knew it was false.

His job was coming to an end. He had been given a new role in another part of the world; this time as personal protection to the consulate in Moscow.

Mike ignored the incoming call from Levison. The bastard could sweat. Mike's last job was to pass the file on to Myers, or whatever his name was, and then he could disappear for a few weeks before moving to Russia unless something changed.

The lab would close soon. No one there had any idea that H.M.G. were pulling the plug. They had everything they needed from their investment and without the government money he doubted the lab would be able to continue. Truth was that the whole project was a fuck up. Yes, they had done what they promised but the end result had turned out to be a nightmare. Mike had already had to clear up one loose end but there'd be more, of that he was in no doubt. He had no qualms about the work he was paid to do but something like this would not end well for anyone connected to it. At least he would be thousands of miles away. Out of sight, out of mind.

## CHAPTER 20

"I know he fucked-up, but he was a good detective, one of the best," Monroe pleaded. The D.C.I. overseeing the enquiry into the murder of the old lady was having none of it.

Monroe had gone straight to the police station to try and lift the pressure of Wise.

"With the greatest respect to you, sir, I think you're too close to Wise to be impartial," Acting Detective Chief Inspector Dan Rickett replied.

Monroe felt insulted. His integrity had never been called into question before. "How dare you…"

Rickett held up his hands. "As I said, sir," he interrupted. "I'm just saying your friendship with Wise is bound to colour your opinion of him. It's just human nature. That's why you've been distanced from the enquiry."

He knew he was right, but Monroe had never really liked Rickett. He was a highflyer, never smoked, never drank alcohol, never swore and was a paragon of political correctness. He was the changing face of the police service, one Monroe and others of his service felt uneasy with.

"I've been given the task of investigating the murder at the flat and the others and that's what I'm going to do. Right now, Wise is our chief suspect in the death of Mildred Moloney. He was seen leaving the old lady's flat and within minutes the place is on fire and she's found dead. Doesn't take a genius to put Wise at the top of our list of suspects that, at this present moment in time, amounts to one name only... John Wise."

Monroe wanted to tell Wise's side of the story but then he'd be admitting to having spoken to him since the old lady's death and that would just open up another pile of shit he could ill afford to wade through just now. He said nothing.

"I've allocated the resources and I'm working on the investigation policy and I'd be grateful for any help you could give me right now, sir."

"I'd help you in any way I can, but I am telling you now that Wise is not responsible for her death."

"And how could you be so sure, sir?" Rickett's eyes narrowed. He knew Monroe was holding something back.

"I can't be sure, of course not, not one-hundred percent, but I do know Wise was working as an advisor to us, at my behest, and he had stumbled on a link to the laboratory. I had already been poking around there and I have an officer on the inside there. When I was warned off the lab by the Commissioner's office, Wise decided he could do the things I couldn't do. Now he's being framed for something he didn't do. Can't you see? It's a set up by someone in power."

Rickett laughed. "Can you hear yourself, sir? Never took you for a conspiracy theorist."

"How dare you," Monroe shouted.

The acting D.C.I. stood. "If you continue in this way, sir, I'll be forced to report your actions to Professional Standards. There's more than enough to get you suspended for a while and that will be long enough to get you out of the way whilst I get hold of Wise. I warn you, interfere in my investigation and you will have to answer for it."

Professional Standards was the department in the police that policed the police. Once called Complaints and Discipline, the officers charged with investigating their colleagues took their job very seriously. They believed they were the guardians of integrity within the service and had little or no qualms about investigating their own. The last thing Monroe needed was to be the focus of one of their teams.

## CHAPTER 21

The motel was a seedy motorway complex of three single storey buildings set in a U-shape on the northbound carriageway of the M1. Martine had headed for the motorway and had followed her brother's directions. They had to keep moving away from London and Wise knew there were many places they could stop if they headed for Scotland. If they made it that far, there were options for ferry crossings to the islands or even further afield. First, they needed to rest.

The sun had already set in the west when Martine switched off the engine and they headed for the reception. The stink of diesel fumes, mixed with petrol, spilled oil, and discarded takeaways that needed clearing turned Martine's stomach. "This place stinks," she complained.

"It's better than sleeping in the car."

The front desk was in the foyer of the centre block. The rooms were indicated by arrows to the left and the right. Behind the reception, Wise could see a bar and a restaurant.

"You'd better book us in under your name," Wise told Martine. "If I use my bank cards it'll flag up our location. Yours might not get flagged for a day or so."

Martine didn't look happy. "I've not got much in my account. Possibly enough for a few days at most."

Wise shrugged. "I'll pay you back. I'll get cash as soon as I can." He fished in his trouser pocket and produced his wallet. He had forty pounds in cash and a few coins. "That's all I've got on me."

Martine stared at the bar. "Enough for me to get pissed tonight, I suppose."

They booked in under Martine's married name and headed for the room. It was small but had twin beds. The bathroom looked like it needed a good steam clean and Martine grimaced. "This place hasn't seen a cleaner in weeks."

"We only need the beds."

Martine walked to the bed furthest from the door and pulled back the duvet. At least the sheets looked clean.

"Let's go get something to eat and a drink," Wise suggested.

"Anything other than being stuck in here longer than absolutely necessary," she agreed.

Wise ordered a cheeseburger and Martine a prawn salad. The food was quick and, whilst not gourmet, was satisfying.

Martine paid the bill with the cash Wise had given her and followed him into the bar.

The bar was large and dimly lit, perfect as far as Wise was concerned. He asked Martine to go to the bar to order the drinks. The less people who saw his face the better. Martine obliged and returned to their corner table with a pint of Guinness for him and a large white wine for herself.

"Best part of nine bloody quid, that was," she moaned.

"At least the meal was cheap."

"Aye, they draw you in with reasonably priced grub and then sting you for the booze."

"Probably don't want people getting pissed in a motorway service station," Wise suggested. "Don't want piss-heads shoot off down the bloody motorway in the morning, do they?"

Martine sighed. "I guess not. No fucking chance at these prices."

They sat quietly, Wise with his back to the corner and with a full view of the bar. Martine sat opposite and said nothing. She was clearly exhausted. Wise smiled. It was great to see her again, even if it wasn't under the best circumstances.

"What are you grinning at?" Martine said. She had drunk most of her large glass of white in one shot. Less than a quarter remained.

"Just thinking it's nice to be with you again."

She shrugged and snorted. "I could think of better ways."

He nodded. "I'm really sorry to get you involved in all this, but I was stuck."

"And the first person you thought of was me, even after everything?"

"Actually, yes. We were always so close."

Martine drained her glass and set it on the table. "I'm sorry I blamed you for Peter's death. I've been thinking it through since you arrived. I know I was wrong, and I know you did what you thought was right and for the right reasons," she smiled too. "Fancy another drink? I'll get it on my card."

Wise swallowed the remains of his pint and placed the glass next to Martine's. As she headed for the bar, Wise noticed a man within a small group nearby, dressed in workers overalls emblazoned with a logo for a heating company. The man was staring at Wise and talking to his mates at the same time. It looked to Wise as if he was talking about him and the others in the group were laughing. Some were looking in Wise's direction whilst one of the group looked uncomfortable or awkward, clearly not comfortable with whatever the gobby man was saying.

The pint had already started to work and Wise needed the toilet. He stood and left his coat over the back of his seat to reserve it, not that there were enough customers to cause a problem. He followed the signs to a corridor behind the bar and entered the gents. Four individual urinals were affixed to the wall and Wise took the furthest. The door opened and the mouthy worker entered. He walked with an arrogance and confidence that Wise knew wasn't deserved. At a little over six foot three, he was taller than Wise and probably weighed in at close to two hundred pounds – at least thirty pounds heavier than himself but the worker's poundage seemed to be huddled mainly around his waist. Wise was still fit and strong and had a ruthless streak that he had always been able to control enough to subdue anyone and everyone he had ever come into conflict with and still have something in reserve.

The worker waltzed up to the urinal next to Wise and stared at him as he began to relive himself. "Fucking hell, what happened to your mush, mate?" He said.

Wise looked at him and then away. He finished and began to wash his hands.

Heater man seemed affronted. "You ignoring me, man, or you just lost your tongue too, along with your face?"

Wise swilled his hands and moved to the dryer.

The heater man finished and zippered up his overalls. "Hey, I was talking to you, just being nice, you ugly fuck."

He could feel the blood pulse in his head and the anger growing, the volcanic magma racing up through his body, heading for the extremities. "Just let it drop while you have a chance," Wise said, controlling his anger better than he expected.

Heater man stepped towards him and spun him around, his face close in to Wise, spittle spraying Wise as he began to rage. "You think you can take me, Frankie? Frankie, know why I call you Frankie? Is that your name or should I call you by your full name Mr Frankenstein?"

Before the burns, Wise would drop the man with a headbutt, but it had become far too painful for that. Instead, he brought up his knee into the man's groin. Heater man winced and doubled over. "You..." he screamed but Wise had already sent a rising left into the side of the man's head. He wobbled but didn't go down. He was holding his groin with his left hand and now thrashing out at Wise with his right.

Wise stepped back and kicked him in the head. That did the trick. The man fell back onto the tiled floor. In the past, that would have been enough, but the volcano had now erupted for the first time in his life. The magma was shooting free and Wise couldn't stop himself. He bent over the man and rained punches at his head. Only when the man lay motionless, bleeding from his eyes, mouth and nose did Wise stop and step back.

He wasn't horrified. He should have been, he should have felt guilt or remorse, but he didn't. He checked the man's pulse. He was alive, just. He had to get rid of the guy before his friends came looking for him. Wise grabbed him under his arm pits and dragged him out of the toilet into the passageway that led from the bar to an emergency exit. He thanked his lucky stars that the bar was pretty empty and that someone had put money into a jukebox. Stairway to Heaven was playing loudly through the speakers and Wise began to laugh. Very appropriate, he thought. This guy was close to climbing those stairs. He bundled the unconscious man out through the emergency exit and into the carpark. Several heavy goods vehicles were parked in a line outside, just a metre or so away from the door. Cab curtains were drawn and the flickering lights inside the cabs suggested the drivers were tucked up, taking their well-deserved rest and watching a little television. Perfect. He lifted the heavy man onto his shoulders and walked to the rear of the first articulated truck. The rear door to the load area was open, a habit all drivers adopted when staying overnight to show prospective thieves that there was nothing inside to steal. Wise hefted the big man into the back of the truck and then climbed up alongside him. He pulled the man into the shadows behind the door that was closed. He jumped down and locked the other shut too.

By the time he returned to the bar, Martine was sipping her wine and a fresh pint of the black stuff was waiting for him.

Wise sat and watched the other men from the heating company. None of them seemed to miss their mate for nearly thirty minutes. Martine had got another round in before one of them could be heard asking where their pal had gone. They clearly weren't that concerned about him. They soon came to a mutual conclusion that he had headed off to bed already.

Wise sipped more of his pint as his headache returned with a vengeance.

## CHAPTER 22

"Three burner phones for sixty quid? That won't be suspicious, will it?" Martine sneered.

"I'm not suggesting you buy three together. One from each shop. I'll get cash and we'll move on straight away, well away from the cashpoint in a direction they won't expect."

They had risen with the sun and Wise took a shower. Martine refused to use the bath but washed herself thoroughly before they strolled to the restaurant for the breakfast included in the price of the room. Three of the workmen were sitting together already and all three were looking worried. They clearly hadn't found their friend.

Martine took a seat at a table in the restaurant and Wise excused himself. He checked the carpark and the lorry containing the unconscious heating man had gone. He began to laugh. He was probably on his way to the driver's next destination.

Wise suddenly stopped laughing. Why was he laughing? It wasn't a laughing matter. The bloke was close to death when he left him and might well have passed away during the night. What was wrong with him, why hadn't he stopped beating on the man and why hadn't he felt remorse? What was happening to him?

They ate breakfast and Wise watched the other heating engineers as they made calls to their friend's phone. If he was still alive, he'd be answering soon, if he had a signal wherever he was. It was time to get the hell out of there.

They finished their plates and headed out to the car just as one of the heating guys got a reply. He heard him shouting into his phone. "Where the hell are you? We've been worried sick, for God's sake."

There was a pause before he spoke again. Wise was closing his door when he heard, "Where? How the hell did you get to Pembroke Dock?" Now Wise grinned.

"What?" Martine asked.

"What, *what*?"

"*What* are you grinning for?"

"Nothing. Let's just get out of here, eh?"

Martine parked the car on a main street through a small town in the north of London. Wise jumped out and used the cashpoint to take three hundred and fifty pounds out of his account – the maximum allowed for his account per day.

Martine found a carpark behind a pub and a twenty-four-hour shop that sold pay-as-you-go phones. She bought one for a penny under twenty pounds and they moved on west towards the next small town. They needed to get the phones quickly and change direction between shops to confuse anyone who might be already tracing his bank transactions. If they discovered their movements, they'd be hard pressed to guess where they were going. They would guess west, but Martine would change direction after the last phone pick up and head north to make it look like they were escaping London.

It took nearly all day to find the last shop selling phones within their limited budget and by that time they were less than fifty miles north of London and in need of another hotel for the night.

## CHAPTER 23

The woman looked nicely presented. Isaac guessed she was probably in her early forties, but she had clearly looked after herself and she could easily pass herself off as ten years younger.

He followed her at a distance through the shopping centre, stopping occasionally to look into shop windows each time she stopped or changed direction. He had been trained for this kind of thing.

The woman was tall, over five-eight and slim. She wore a black low-cut top and short leather skirt over black tights and red heels. Her long red hair was tied into a ponytail that reached the top of her skirt. Isaac had heard men describe women of her age as mutton dressed as lamb but there was nothing mutton about this woman. She oozed class. Even her walk was sexy. She wasn't on his 'to-do list' but he had the urge and it wouldn't hurt to throw the coppers off his real reason for killing, not that he needed one. The 'list' was a project, something that potentially could make him the most prolific killer in history.

The woman turned the heads of men, and some women, as she walked through the Saturday evening shoppers. Isaac checked his watch; eight o'clock. The shopping centre would be clearing soon as they prepared to shut the place in thirty minutes time. Not long to go now. He could feel the excitement building, an ache, a real physical ache to release on his target. She wouldn't know what hit her. He began to chuckle as he watched he checked her own watch and head towards a pub outside the shopping centre. He followed her inside.

The bar was crowded, full of shoppers taking a well-earned rest from their self-imposed toil and dozens of men in Chelsea football shirts celebrating a win earlier in the day.

Isaac pushed through the crowd to the bar and moved up behind the woman. She was attempting to attract the attention of the barman. He took a deep breath, inhaling her scent, there was something about her smell. Something he hadn't picked up when she walked past him in the shopping centre. The smell bothered him. He had always trusted his senses and now he was confused. He moved alongside his target as she ordered a gin and tonic. "I'll get that," he smiled through perfect, white teeth.

"No need, I've got it," the woman smiled back.

"Let me. I've had a good day and I'm celebrating," he insisted.

"Really? I'm happy for you, but there's no need."

"It's no trouble." He handed a fifty-pound note to the barman and asked for a glass of champagne for himself.

"Wow. You must have had a good day," the woman said.

"Just been offered a promotion. It's a very good day," Isaac added.

"You work in the city?"

"How can you tell?"

"No one else would order champagne in a pub."

"Ah, too flash?" he said.

She laughed. "No, not at all, well, maybe just a little."

Isaac laughed too. "My name's Charles, but I like to be called Charlie." He held out his hand.

"Hayley, I like to be called Hayley."

Isaac laughed again. "Pleased to meet you, Hayley."

"Likewise, and thanks for the drink." Hayley took a gulp and looked around the bar.

"I think they're celebrating," Isaac said.

"What makes you think that?" Hayley laughed again.

"I've decided I'm going to celebrate tonight… big time. Would you care to join me?"

Hayley blushed. "You don't even know me."

"I know your name is Hayley and that you're a stunningly beautiful woman. What more do I need to know?"

"Do you say these things to every woman you meet?"

He shook his head and drank some champagne. "No, only the very few stunning ones I meet and believe me, they are few and far between."

"You've been practicing your chat up lines," Hayley said and looked away, seemingly unimpressed.

Isaac heard the alarm in his head. He was losing her. He had to do something quick or he'd blow out. "Sorry," he sighed. "I'm really not as confident as I might seem. I guess I'm compensating."

"For what?" Now Hayley turned back to him and grinned.

Isaac laughed. "Not that, for sure."

Hayley nodded. "Look, I appreciate the interest, I really do, but you're not my type."

"Oh? And what would your type be?"

She shrugged. Probably blonde with long legs, breasts and no penis."

His eyes widened. How the hell had he misjudged her? He should have trusted his senses.

"You're surprised? Not all us lesbians have cropped and dyed hair and dress like a man."

He held up his hands. He checked his watch, time was running out. This was a lost cause. He had to move on. "Sorry," he finally said. "What a waste."

Hayley felt infuriated. How dare he? "Excuse me?" she growled but Isaac had already finished his drink and walked off into the crowd.

## CHAPTER 24

Sitting at the back of the briefing, Monroe felt uncomfortable. He had not been welcome but had insisted he would observe Rickett's handling of the murder of the old lady. He wanted to know everything Rickett and his team knew to ensure he and Wise stayed ahead of the game.

"Right, ladies and gentlemen, settle down," Rickett said. He stood at the front of a group of ten detectives in a briefing room on the top floor of Lime Street Police Station. A large glass screen stood on aluminium legs behind him, illuminated by L.E.D. lights in the frame, the marker pens used would glow and provide a clear reading for all assembled. A large blow-up photograph of Mildred was taped to the glass. "This is Mildred Moloney. Aged eighty-six. She lived alone in a top floor apartment opposite where our former colleague John Wise used to live. We know Wise's apartment was the subject of a fire. The place was destroyed, along with the neighbouring properties. It seems, from initial reports from the Fire Service, that an improvised explosive device was used in Wise's flat. Does this mean Wise was the target or..." he paused for effect. "...has Wise lost the plot. We know he's had a turbulent three years. So, was

Wise the manufacturer of the device and did it blow-up on him by mistake?"

Monroe wanted to shout 'bollocks' but held his tongue.

"If Wise did make the device, what the hell was it intended for? The acid attack might have screwed his head, and we also know that Wise was seen leaving Mrs Moloney's apartment minutes before the discovery of another fire at her apartment and the body being found inside. I'm awaiting the PM. I've been informed that it'll be later today, and I hope to give you an update on the results as soon as they are available to me. Unfortunately, two other bodies were found in the apartments next to Wise's and they are currently under the knife."

A Krosonofski, a wizened detective in a crumpled grey suit raised his hand. "Why the hell would Wise do something like this? I worked with him for nearly twenty years. Even after the acid thing I can't see him losing it like this."

Rickett bristled at the comments. "Let me tell you all now, if anyone lets personal feelings get in the way of a thorough investigation because of misplaced loyalty," he said and glanced briefly at Monroe, "I'll make sure your arse is out the door quicker than you can say 'but sir,' do you all understand?"

Mumbles of acknowledgement were the best Rickett could expect. He knew there were two teams in play – those who liked and admired Wise and those who seemingly hated him. The hate camp was in the ascendance and whilst Rickett had sufficient suspicion now to bring Wise in for questioning, he had been in the 'admire' camp until the death of the old lady. He really hoped he was innocent, as Monroe insisted. The fact that Wise had now done a runner suggested otherwise. It didn't look good for Wise and Rickett would do everything he could to bring him in.

Monroe sat quietly at the rear of the assembly. Rickett made a point of not looking at him again. He went through the briefing in a professional manner, just like any other enquiry and seemingly keen to make an example of Wise – the ex-copper – if he was guilty.

It didn't make for happy listening. Monroe understood Rickett. He was a good and solid detective, much like Wise himself, but whereas Wise had always had his faults, Rickett seemed to go out of his way each day in proving he had none. At just five foot six, he wouldn't have been accepted as a police officer in most of the constabularies and forces around the UK a decade or two ago, he would have been considered too short, but times had changed. Senior officers had recognised that size didn't matter when it came to intelligence and determination, physical toughness and resolve. But not all the changes had been welcome for the dinosaurs like Monroe and Wise. They both made it known that they both despised the new political correctness and the willingness and even eagerness on the part of the new breed to shop a colleague for not doing everything by the book. It was being done in what was considered to be the 'right thing', but the erosion of trust had become pervasive. Monroe and Wise had been part of a team where they would literally watch each other's backs. They had been a team where they looked after each other and even put their lives and reputations on the line for each other. That attitude had been destroyed by policies to employ senior officers with little or no experience of walking the streets, of facing the knives and spitting drunks, and it didn't matter how good the new breed of officer was at managing resources, they would never understand the world of the officers who were out there doing the job, and those members of the thin blue line that were doing the job at the sharp end resented that ignorance.

## CHAPTER 25

The Grand House Hotel was nestled in several acres of ancient, protected woodland. A long winding driveway twisted and undulated between regimental lines of majestic oaks as Martine drove the car towards the converted Elizabethan building.

"How are we going to afford this?" Martine asked. "It looks like bloody Downton Abbey."

"We'll use your credit card."

"Oh, that's nice of you to offer my card."

Martine said nothing more as they neared the house. A large parking area of small white stones fronted the main entrance and dozens of cars were parked in lines. Martine found a gap in one of the lines and parked the car. "Looks like there's something on."

"It's a big place. Might still be room.?"

The hotel had been found on Martine's phone. Wise had Googled for hotels in their areas and Grand House was the closest to them. Wise was shattered. They needed somewhere to lie low for the night and a busy hotel was always good for blending into the background, not that Wise could ever really blend in anywhere.

They used Martine's Visa card to pay for a room in a new annex block at the rear of the hotel. The main building was spectacular. All the original features appeared to be intact. High ceilings, ornate covings, exquisitely embroidered drapes and wood panelled walls portrayed an era of opulence and grandeur that mirrored the cost of a room for the night. Martine grimaced at the charge but smiled when she saw a bride in a long white dress enter the reception area with her bridesmaids. "A wedding party?"

As the bride got closer, Martine saw her left cheek had undergone some kind of trauma surgery. The scar had been covered over with makeup but was still visible. The bride saw Wise and smiled at him. "Hello," she said. "Are you with David's side?"

Wise shook his head. "Sorry, no. We're just staying here for the night." Then Wise saw six men dressed in military uniforms, all were officers and three were facially disfigured and the other three were amputees.

"This is David," the bride said as she took a tall handsome man's arm. David was a Captain in the Royal Artillery.

"Nice to meet you," Wise said.

"I thought you were one of the friends from the hospital," the bride said.

"No. I got this from an acid attack when I was a policeman," Wise explained.

"There's not a good whole one between us," David said. "Some of us served together and we met the others when we were recovering after returning from Afghanistan. Had I not lost my arm I'd never have met Pauline," he said as he kissed his bride.

"I got this from shrapnel," Pauline said as she pointed to her cheek. "Looks like you're one of us. You'll fit in well. Come on in. Join the party. We've all had the reception and the band are about to play. Please come and join us."

Martine seemed keen and Wise agreed. They freshened up in the annex room, one of a dozen newly decorated rooms in a block that had once been a stable. The receptionist had told them the story of the hotel and the renovations and the room was decorated to the same style as the main house.

A Fleetwood Mac tribute band was halfway through their first song when Wise and Martine entered the function room that had once been a ballroom. A dozen round tables were dressed in white cloths with lace trimmings. Each hardback chair was similarly decorated to match, and stunning bouquets of flowers stood proudly in the centre of each table. A single red Poppy had been included in each of the bouquets and Wise guessed they were a tribute to those friends and colleagues that David and Pauline had lost during their service with the army. The lights were dimmed, with spotlights illuminating the band, and Wise immediately felt at home. For the first time in three years no one paid him more than a cursory glance. The place was full of people scarred like him. The guests seemed more interested in Martine. Martine was tall and slim, and her strawberry blonde hair had been brushed out into full waves. Her pale skin emphasised against the colour of her flowing locks.

David the Captain made a beeline for them as they stood by the bar. "All the drinks are on the house," he smiled.

"That's very generous," Wise said.

"Got to look after my fellow monsters," he said with a beaming smile. "Don't be offended by the way I talk," he said. "We call ourselves the Monster Mash, after that song. It's our way of dealing with the things that have happened to us. I lost my arm in an I.E.D. nearly ten years ago. Pauline was injured in the same blast. She was a medic in the unit. I was her boss at the time, but we got to know each other during recovery and the rest, as they say, is history. The rest of them are friends we made over the years. They all suffered some kind of injury, loss or trauma and I guess our friendships were built on common ground."

"That's wonderful," Martine said.

"It is now. It took us all a long time to adjust. Life is more than just our appearance."

Wise knew he was right but had always had difficulty in thinking so positively.

David excused himself to talk to another guest and Wise ordered a Guinness for himself and a gin and tonic for Martine.

They found a pair of empty seats in the corner of the hall and listened to the band. Several of the guests were determined to get them to join them on the dancefloor and by midnight they were the worsest for copious amounts of free alcohol and so said goodnight to their new friends.

\*\*\*

The white Transit van was heading for a postcode to the north of London. Godfrey had received a call from a source to say that a credit card registered to the sister of John Wise had been used to book a room at a hotel. He had asked for updates on cards and cashpoint usage for Wise and his sister. It had made sense to keep tabs on both since Wise had last been in her company and Wise would expect his cards to be monitored but probably not realise his sister's were being watched too. Godfrey had been right.

They got to the hotel just before five am and sat in the van on the road near the entrance to the driveway, watching for any sign of their targets.

\*\*\*

Martine moaned as Wise drew back the curtains and the morning light flooded the hotel room. She had overdone the gin and the champagne consumption during the wedding party and was now paying the price. Wise had drunk several pints of beer but felt good. No headache, no nausea, he had escaped the fate of his sister. "Come on, Martine, time for breakfast before we head off again."

"Do we have to?" she groaned.

"If we want to stay ahead of the game then yes, I'm afraid we do."

"I feel like shit," she said as she sat up in her bed.

"I'm not surprised," Wise grinned. "You devoured the champers like it was going out of fashion."

"I only had one or two," she protested.

"Aye, one or two bottles."

Martine swung her legs out from under the covers and moaned again as she tried to stand. "Oh shit. I think I'm going to be sick."

Only a handful of the wedding guests were up for breakfast. The self-service options had been as good as anything Wise had experienced before.

Satiated, Martine handed the key card in to reception. The young woman behind the counter didn't look up as she dropped it onto the desk.

"We need to change our car," Wise said.

"And how are we going to do that, steal one?"

"What a good idea," Wise grinned.

Martine stopped and spun him around to face her. "I was joking."

"What do you suggest then?"

"We could hire one."

"How long do you think it'll take for us to be traced in a hire car?"

As they walked out of the hotel an old man pulled up in a new B.M.W. five-thirty. He stepped from his car and popped the boot. Before Wise could say anything, Martine walked over to the man and took his case. "Welcome, sir," she said. "Follow me. I'll take you to reception."

She took his case and wheeled it towards the desk.

"Thank you," he said. He handed Martine a ten-pound tip and she smiled.

"I'll park your car and leave the key at reception for you."

The old gent handed the key to her and she walked back out to Wise.

"New ride. I guess you're right about the hire car. I feel like shit but needs must, I suppose."

Wise grinned. "This is a side of you I haven't seen before. You were always the good kid."

She grimaced. "Shut up and just get in." Martine gunned the three-litre engine and slipped it into drive. "He'll get it back safely. We'll leave it at the next place we stop, and he won't lose his no-claims bonus."

"Famous last words."

"Shut up. I feel bad about it as it is. I just need to be careful."

Martine drove, Wise had rarely driven since he had been burnt by the acid. He had never liked driving, unlike Martine. Martine had always loved cars and had even spent several weekends driving high-powered supercars. It made sense for her to take the wheel.

\*\*\*

Tired of waiting, the Transit pulled into the hotel car park just as Wise and Martine were leaving in a pale blue B.M.W.. Doug spotted them as they drove out of the one-way system that accessed the car park.

"That's them," he shouted.

Godfrey continued ~~on~~ into the turning circle and swung the van around in the drive.

He took up position ~~fell in~~ several vehicles behind the ~~BMW~~ B.M.W. as it headed south towards Hendon.

"We'll have to find a way to stop them," Doug said.

"No shit, Sherlock? Give me a chance to think."

The ~~BMW~~ B.M.W. had headed back towards London and the Transit followed behind at a distance. They stopped at traffic lights in the middle of Golders Green and Godfrey moved out into the lane dedicated for right turns at the crossroads. "Fuck it," he said as he stamped down on the accelerator and crashed through a gap into the traffic and careered towards the ~~BMW~~ B.M.W..

"Jesus!" Martine shouted as she saw the Transit heading straight for them in the rear-view mirror, the cars in both lines behind her being thumped aside, horns blaring, glass and broken plastic flying into the air as metal panels buckled and twisted under the force of the determined van.

Wise saw Martine stamp on the gas. The ~~BMW~~ B.M.W. took off into the junction against the red signal.

Car horns sounded again, accompanied by the screech of tyres as cars with the right of way braked hard to avoid the miscreant Beemer. Wise grabbed the handle above his head and pulled his legs up out of the footwell as Martine slid the car around to the left, narrowly missing an oncoming service bus.

"Jesus!" Wise shouted as he closed his eyes and waited for the inevitable crash, but it didn't come, not yet anyway. Martine let the back-end slide and eased off the gas as she steered gently into the skid. The car straightened and she aimed it down the inside of the big red double-decker. The B.M.W. mounted a low kerb and bounced over a drain cover before she pulled the wheel left and the car thumped back onto the road. Cars ahead were stopping, the nose-diving vehicles screeching in protest. Martine cut across the carriageway in front of them and back onto the correct side of the road just as the Transit fell in behind. Vehicles ahead were now slowing, and Martine had nowhere to go. The Transit caught up and, without slowing down, rammed into the back of the Beemer. The impact whipped at the necks of Martine and Wise and both cursed as she floored the accelerated once more and aimed for the pavement to her left. A handful of pedestrians scattered as she clipped the rear corner of a bright red Ferrari and drove up onto a wide footpath leading towards a street of shops.

"That's fucked the old man's no-claims," Wise shouted over the roar of the accelerating B.M.W..

She checked her mirror and saw the Transit had done more than just clip the Ferrari. The red car was smashed up into the air and began to roll away. She could see the driver duck below the screen as the car tumbled over before resting on its side against a lamppost.

"Watch for the doors of the shops!" Wise shouted.

"I know!" she shouted back just as a woman and a child stepped from a doorway right into the path of the B.M.W. now doing close to fifty miles per hour. Martine knew that if she hit them it would be game over for them all. She braked hard and was struck by the van again as she pulled the wheel to the right.

Wise saw the look of horror on the mother's face as her brain began to process the fact that both she and her child were about to die. But Martine's reactions were quicker than those of the pedestrians. Her years of fun behind the wheel of high-powered cars had sharpened her reflexes and the B.M.W. swung back to the left as the rear had been destined to strike the mother and child. Instead, the rear of the car followed the momentum of the input through the steering wheel and the car shot past the two terrified shoppers with just an inch or so to spare.

"Bloody hell! That was close," Wise shouted. Martine nodded just once and dropped down a gear as she accelerated once again.

The van was still rocking and swaying from the earlier impact with the rear of the Beemer and Godfrey was overcompensating as he turned the wheel first one way and then the other. Finally, he realised he needed to ease off the power even if it did mean he'd lose ground on Wise. The van slowed as it passed the mother and child staring in horror.

Martine had the engine of the ~~BMW~~B.M.W. red lining each time she changed up through the six-speed automatic gearbox. The road opened onto a dual carriageway and she smiled as she saw the Transit van dropping back by the second.

Wise could see the tower block that marked the location of Hendon Police Training College. There had been three similar towers at the time he trained there. The centre had closed for a while during major renovations and the college was not like it had been during his time.

Wise stared at the Hendon site as they tore along the road, his mind transported back to those times as a raw recruit when he first wore the uniform of a Metropolitan Police Constable and the enormous sense of pride he felt that day. Then he felt the car begin to slow and he heard Martine curse under her breath.

He looked to the front and saw a line of stationary traffic ahead. He saw Martine check her mirror. "Are they behind us?" he asked.

"No, but it won't be long before they are again," she said.

Martine kept her foot on the brake as it slowed up behind the traffic until it finally came to a stop. Martine kept checking the mirror and drumming out an impatient beat on the steering wheel. Then she grimaced. "There they are," she said.

Wise turned in his seat to look out through the cracked rear window. The Transit van was hurtling up behind them.

## CHAPTER 26

The man walked slowly through the extensive grounds of a large house. A lake occupied nearly three acres of the eight-acre site and all garden paths wound down to a star-shaped junction with another arm leading down to the lake and following the kidney shaped circumference of the still, green waters. Flowers had been strategically planted in places that were meant to make them look entirely natural. The inmates had all worked hard on the garden as part of their rehabilitation. Palm trees had grown to nearly five metres in the protection of the hollow that played host to the lake. Caine remembered planting one of them twenty-odd years ago. He smiled as he remembered the others that had worked with him at that time. Most had gone now, either back to prison to serve out a sentence or released, or even dead. Caine had no chance of ever being released but not because he was deemed to be a danger to society, but because he did not want to ever be released. This was the only place he truly felt safe.

Brompton Abbey had been built by Cistercian Monks in the eleventh century. The main, original building had been no bigger than many middle-class homes today but was sufficient for the accommodation of a dozen monks at that time. A

Church had been built aligned to the traditional east-west layout and had been a plain stone structure with little adornment that had seemed to become common place within the Catholic religion over the centuries. Another accommodation block had been added on the opposite side of the main building in later years and then the order suffered at the hands of the reformation. Henry the VIII had given the abbey and the land to one of his most loyal generals in the last years of the monarch's reign. Since then, it had changed hands many times but always remained as a private home until nineteen-sixty-eight. That was the year the abbey became an asylum and it wasn't until nearly twenty years after that that Caine became a resident.

Caine walked tall with a minor permanent limp after an infection in his left leg had eaten away the heel of his foot. Surgeons had no choice but to amputate the foot. The limp was barely noticeable and more prominent first thing in the morning. He kept fit by walking and running and weight training. He had taken to prosthetics so well that, eight years ago, he had been approached by a coach for the British para-Olympic team. Caine had no interest in sport and politely declined.

He stood at the edge of the lake and watched a pair of Mallard ducks swim towards a small island at the far side where Caine knew they nested. There'd be no baby ducks for another six months or so and Caine couldn't wait to see the little creatures again. There was something about ducks he loved. Perhaps it was the fact that their legs remained beneath the surface and they looked perfectly normal above the water. Perhaps it was the fake freedom they shared with Caine. Caine was allowed to roam the grounds and go accompanied to town on occasions, but his wings had been clipped, just like those of the ducks. At least, officially he was restricted to the house, but there had been a long-standing agreement that was never talked about, nor was it ever questioned. Caine had spent his early years in the company of the super wealthy and politically powerful and those links had served him well since his confinement.

The smell of wild garlic made his stomach rumble. He had eaten a good breakfast of muesli and fruit, but nothing compared to a full English; it was just that his blood pressure had been high of late and the doctor had advised against too much fat. He walked back up towards the abbey and the open kitchen window where the fried food was still being served. He leaned in through the window as Beverley, the cook was frying eggs on the nearby stove. "Chuck a couple on for me, please, Bev," he shouted and laughed as Beverley jumped.

"Jesus Christ, Caine. You'll give me a sodding heart attack and, talking of heart attacks, aren't you supposed to stay off the fried food?"

He grinned. "We only live once."

She smiled back and shrugged her shoulders. "~~Okay~~OK, your funeral. Full English, is it?"

"Oh yes, eggs over easy and bacon crispy."

She grinned. "I know how you like it," she turned to face him and pulled down the zipper on her white chef's jacket. Caine knew she never wore a bra and her ample breasts spilled out before him.

Caine laughed. "You better put those away until later," he winked.

"Promises, promises," she teased.

Beverley loved teasing Caine and knew he loved it too. The teasing had developed into something far more intimate some months ago and Caine had turned out to be an insatiable lover, something she was grateful for. Her husband had cheated on her pretty much from the first day of their marriage. She had discovered that her had even fucked one of the bridesmaids at the wedding whilst she was mingling with guests. It wasn't until she first saw the extremely good-looking Caine Conran, nearly fifteen years after her wedding, that she too was tempted to stray. She knew all about him. She knew that he would always be a resident at the facility, but she also knew he was considered 'safe.' He was calm thanks to a cocktail of drugs that purged him of the demons that had pushed him over the edge as a young man. He had confided in her after that the first time they had made love. She grinned at the thought of that first time. It could never truly be called making love. They had flirted for a while and then, one morning, after she had cleared the breakfast things for the fifteen residents at the facility, Caine had entered the kitchen and begun kissing her. Things quickly progressed and then she found herself bent over the sink being fucked by the inmate. The excitement was enhanced for her by the fact that the inmates had all been classified as potentially dangerous. Caine was certainly not dangerous; other than he packed a deadly weapon in his pants. She grinned again at the thought of that morning and of the dozens of times each week he had taken her in some bizarre location or position.

"Don't bother with the sausage," Caine said. "I've already got one."

She laughed. "I know."

## CHAPTER 27

The van slowed to match the pace of the other traffic. The B.M.W. was in the nearside lane behind a car as it stopped for a red light. A right-only lane was also occupied by two cars and Godfrey saw his chance. He pulled in the righthand lane and accelerated at the gap between the two lines of traffic. It had worked well the first time and this time Godfrey would make sure he stopped the B.M.W. – permanently.

The crash of metal and blaring of horns as the van smashed through the cars had Martine checking her mirrors once more.

"Jesus. Don't they give up?"

Wise half turned in his seat and shouted, "Go."

"Shit!"

The van had caused devastation at both junctions. People were screaming and shouting at the vehicles. One man threw a can of Cole at the B.M.W. and the projectile crashed into the windscreen, causing a large crack to appear. "Shit, there's goes the old man's screen cover," Wise said.

The B.M.W. found a gap into the traffic and veered between the cars ahead. The van followed close behind and made ground on them as the Beemer slowed again for another junction.

"Don't stop," Wise shouted just as the van crashed into the back of them. The boot crumpled and the rear screen shattered into millions of tiny pieces that pelted the front of the van. The front screen of the van had shattered in the impact too and Doug kicked his heavy boot through it to clear it from the frame.

The B.M.W. raced through a gap in the traffic crossing before them and the van collided with a red baker's van as Godfrey punched out the last fragments of glass that were obscuring his view.

The road was too narrow to gun the Beemer any faster. The van closed the gap again and hit the rear once more. Wise turned to see Doug launch himself out through the windscreen and land on the buckled boot of the car. The big man crawled into the back and grabbed at Martine's throat. Wise punched him in the face again and again until he let go of his sister. Then the world turned upside down as a small truck side-swiped the B.M.W. Wise heard his sister scream then everything went black.

The car rolled and came to a stop on its roof.

He knew he hadn't been unconscious for long because he awoke to find himself hanging from his seat belt like a stunned vampire bat.

Wise raised his hand and ran it over his body from his head to his legs. There was nothing broken and no blood. He turned his head slowly to look at his sister. She was hanging beside him with a nasty gash on her forehead that was dripping blood onto the headlining of the roof. He touched her face. The skin was warm. He checked her pulse. It was slow but regular.

"Martine?" His sister stirred. That was a good sign. She could hear him.

A voice to his left startled him. "You alright, mate? Jesus, what happened to your face?"

Wise looked at the uniformed police officer kneeling by his door. "It's an old injury. I'm ~~okay~~OK." Wise thought he saw a flash of recognition on the copper's face. Had he connected the face with the wanted man he had become?

"Just hang on there until the ambulance arrives. Don't move."

"Taking the piss or what?" Wise could hear the siren approaching nearby. "How's the big guy in the back?"

"What big guy?" the policeman said as he peered past Wise.

Wise turned his head slowly, careful not to cause himself an injury. The big man had gone. He must have escaped before the police arrived.

"Where the hell am I?" Martine mumbled. "My head hurts."

"Don't move. We're hanging upside down. Stay there until the ambulance crew help you out."

Martine moved her head and groaned as she saw the policeman.

A second uniformed officer appeared at Martine's side. "Don't worry love. We'll get you out. There's no real risk of fire. This is a diesel. It has a higher flashpoint."

"That's encouraging," she said sarcastically.

The sound of the siren was deafening as the ambulance pulled to a stop nearby. The policeman stood and walked away. Wise guessed he was going to liaise with the crew.

"You've got to get away," Martine said. "They'll arrest you and then you'll be knackered."

"I can't leave you here, not like this."

"I'll be OK. Go, while you have the chance."

Wise knew she was right and that he had no option other than to run if he didn't want to spend the next day or so in a police cell. "I'll find out where they take you and I'll come and get you," he said but Martine had lost consciousness again. Wise pressed the button on the seat belt catch and he fell to the roof with a thump and a groan.

By the time the coppers returned to the car with the ambulance crew Wise was already at the end of the street hiding in a doorway.

\*\*\*

Godfrey and Doug stood at the junction of the main road with an alley that ran behind the high street shops. They watched the police and ambulance crew and saw Wise make a run for it. They were too far away to go after him without being seen, so they stayed still. They still had his sister in view, and they knew Wise would not be far away. They could hail a cab and follow the ambulance and wait for Wise to turn up there. Godfrey made a quick search for a taxi company on his phone and made a note of the number. The van was totalled, and a taxi wasn't ideal, but he knew the nearest hire car outlet was over three miles away. He held off on the call. He wanted to see what would develop.

## CHAPTER 28

"Excuse me," an old lady said as she pushed past Wise in the narrow doorway. He turned to find he was standing outside a café. He opened the door and took an empty table next to the window. He could just see the front end of the B.M.W. from his seat.

A waitress walked up to the table. "Nasty accident," she said nodding to the carnage down the street and smiled and then recoiled at the sight of his face. Realising she had embarrassed him and herself, the waitress sat on an empty seat opposite Wise. "I'm sorry," she said.

"For what?"

"For that look… you know."

"Don't worry, it happens all the time. I'm used to it."

"No, seriously. I'm really sorry. I should know better."

Wise was intrigued. "Oh?"

The waitress untied the knot at her neck that secured her apron and let it drop. She lifted her T-shirt and exposed a large burn scar across her waist. "You show me yours and I'll show you mine," she smiled.

Wise laughed and took a sly look out the window. The two police officers were looking around the scene, probably looking for him. They split up and one took the far pavement and the other the nearest. They started walking in the direction of the café. "I'm sorry," he said.

She shook her head. "I've had years of adjusting to it. Yours looks quite new."

"Three years and two days," he agreed.

"Mine is a water burn. I pulled a boiling kettle over me as a child. What about you?"

"Acid. I was a copper and some bastard threw it in my face."

She winced. "Bastard."

She held out her right hand. "I'm Samantha," she said, "please call me Sam."

He shook her hand. "John. My friends call me Wise."

"And are you? Wise I mean."

He laughed. "I wish. It's my surname."

He looked at the waitress and found himself attracted to her. Her long blonde hair was tied back in a ponytail. She was not what he or anyone else would consider to be a classical beauty. Her nose was slim but slightly too long for her face and her features were asymmetrical but attractive because of that. A light dusting of bronze eyeshadow and a little lip gloss was all the makeup she wore but Wise didn't think she needed anything to enhance her. He checked the road again and the coppers were closer now. If they kept walking, they would be at the café in less than fifteen minutes. The only thing slowing them were the checks they were making in the other shops and windows as they progressed.

Sam saw him looking and sighed. "Don't tell me you're wanted by the police?"

He thought about lying to her, but the officers would be in the café soon and then he'd be nicked and whisked away in handcuffs. "For something I didn't do," he said.

"Don't they all say that?" she replied, unsure.

"I guess so. But it's true. My sister and I were rammed off the road by the two men who killed an old lady. I had been with her before she was killed, and the bastards have set me up for it. I swear to you I didn't do it. She was a lovely lady. She had helped me." He went on to quickly explain his involvement with the investigation into the murders and how he had been tied to a chair in his flat by the men who had rammed the B.M.W. He told her about the bomb and how he had escaped and ended up in Mildred's flat.

Sam said nothing, just nodding occasionally. She stared at him for a moment then spoke. "OK. I believe you. I have no idea why, but I do. You need to go out the back door now. I have a moped out the back. You can use it."

Wise was shocked. "Seriously?"

"Come on, you'd be useless as a criminal with your face like that," she joked. She stood and hurried to a door leading to the office at the back of the café. Wise followed her and she took a crash helmet from a metal locker and handed it to him. "Here. Use this." She gave him a keyring with two keys on it, and a card. "That's got my home address on it, there is directions on the back, and my house key is on the keyring. Go there and wait until I finish up here. I'll be here until five. Can you cook?"

"I do a wicked Bolognese," he said.

"You can pay me back by cooking me dinner. All the stuff you need is in the kitchen. Now go."

Wise squeezed his head into the helmet. It was a tight fit and hurt his face. He left through the back door into an enclosed yard. The moped was an old model but started on the button. He rode the bike out onto a service lane and headed towards the main road.

***

"That's him!" Godfrey said as Wise rode past on a moped. "Where the hell did he get that?" Godfrey made a note of the registration number and grinned. "Time to make another call," he said.

## CHAPTER 29

It took Wise ten minutes to reach the apartment block. The building was a huge rectangular structure of red brick. Six floors of apartments with balconies overlooked the main road. At the centre of the front face was a large entrance to an underground car park. Wise rode the moped down the ramp and into the dimly lit space. Dozens of spaces were vacant and an area at one end, near a lift, was designated for motorcycles. Wise left the bike in one of the bays and took the lift to the third floor. Sam's apartment was the third door along the corridor. All the doors were to his left and a wall of windows out to the rear communal garden are was to his right.

He used the key to enter. The key was worn and needed a little jiggling, but he got it open and entered a well-appointed one-bedroom flat. The hall floor was tiled, and the aroma of a plug-in air freshener was almost overpowering. At the end of the short hallway was a kitchen and a compact living room. A door to his left led to the only bedroom and the door to the right opened into a modern bathroom.

Wise dropped the crash helmet onto a pale grey leather settee that was angled to face a patio door leading onto the small balcony. A television set stood on an aluminium coffee table in one corner.

Using Sam's telephone, Wise tapped in Monroe's number and he answered on the third ring.

"Thank God, you're OK. The police are looking for you again."

"Good luck with that," he said. "Any news on Martine?"

"She's been taken to the local hospital. She's fine. She'll have an x-ray on her head, but it looks OK. She'll be kept in overnight for observations. Stay away from the hospital for a day or so. Martine has been arrested for T.D.A." Taking and Driving Away was the charge that both men had known well during their early policing career. During the early days theft of vehicles for joyriding had been on an epidemic scale.

"I need to see her."

"I understand that. Look, I'll call in to see her tomorrow. I'll tell the P.C. on duty there that I'm relieving him out the goodness of my heart."

"He won't believe that."

"Then I'll pull rank. While he's gone you can pop in and see her for a few minutes. I need to tell you something too, but not over the phone."

"I'll ring you tomorrow morning."

He set the kettle to boil and looked through the cupboards to find the ingredients he needed for the Bolognese. Satisfied all was as it should be, he prepared the ingredients, set his alarm in case he fell asleep then collapsed onto the settee and watched some daytime television.

The alarm on his watch buzzed and woke him at four in the afternoon. He had slept for hours and still felt exhausted. He fiddled with the cooker until he was happy with the controls and then put the food on to cook. A bottle of red wine had been opened and was reclining in a wire rack on the countertop. He took the bottle and placed it in the centre of a small round dining table next to the settee. Two hard chairs were pushed back against the wall to maximise space in the small lounge and he positioned one each side of the table. He had everything prepared just in time for Sam's return. He heard the knock at the door and checked through the spyhole. Sam stood there with a cardboard box. She had obviously seen a movement behind the door and opened the lid on the box to reveal two chocolate eclairs and a broad smile.

"I come baring gifts," she said as he opened the door.

"Grubs up," he smiled.

They sat together and ate in silence. The meal was nothing special but still good and they finished the bottle of red before Sam opened another. Wise helped clear up and loaded the dirty dishes into the dishwasher.

Sam switched off the television and slipped a C.D. into a player. She kept the volume low as they moved to the settee and sat at either end.

"So, tell me more about this mess you're in," she said.

He sighed and nodded slowly, contemplating his response. "Guess I owe you the full story," he said as he began to tell her the story again, but this time everything, from the acid attack, his split with the police, the recent murders and the death of the old woman. Sam listened intently and didn't interrupt.

Sam then told him about the café, how she was the now the owner after having worked there most of her life. The old lady who had owned the place, her maternal auntie, had treated her like a daughter and left the café to her in her will. Sam's own mother had not left her with anything other pain. Her dad had left the family home after Sam's accident, blaming her mother for the injuries she had sustained. Sam knew her dad had other reasons to leave; he had a lover and her accident had been the excuse he had needed to cut the ties. Whilst Sam had recovered from her injuries and learned to live with her scars, her mother had never recovered. She too blamed herself for not protecting her daughter and sank into a deep depression that eventually led to her taking her life on the day before Sam's fifth birthday. It was then that

Auntie Aggie had stepped in and adopted her as her own. From the moment she was old enough to work, Sam had helped her aunt in the café, quickly learning the ropes and becoming indispensable.

When they had finished talking, she took his hand and led him to the bedroom. "It's been a long time," she explained. "The last guy nearly freaked when he saw the mess on me. I hope you won't do the same?"

Wise took her in his arms and kissed her softly. "You sure this doesn't put you off?" he said.

"What, your face? I hadn't noticed," she joked as he pushed her onto the bed.

## CHAPTER 30

The house was not what Monroe expected. In truth, he had no idea what kind of house the director of a government laboratory would live in. Levison either didn't make a lot of money or he liked to horde it. He certainly wasn't a man who liked to flash his cash. Number 18 was a mid-terrace house that in any town or city outside of London would cost no more than a hundred thousand pounds. Of course, London was unlike any other town or city when it came to property prices. The yellow glow from the sodium streetlights reflected amber in the scattered pools of rain that had stopped as he arrived at the house. Each property was fronted by a rise of three stone steps leading to the front doors. Levison's door looked like it had recently been painted a pillar box red. Monroe could even smell the paint as he stepped up and knocked on the door. He checked his watch as he waited for a reply. It was nearly ten in the evening and someone was clearly at home. Monroe could see through a small gap in the curtain of the living room and watched as a shadow passed the television set and headed out into the hallway.

"Yes, who is it?" a male voice shouted through the stained-glass front door.

"Doctor Levison? It's the police. I'd like a quick word please."

The door opened on a security chain and Monroe saw the bespectacled man appraise him before speaking. "How can I help you?"

Monroe held out his warrant card for Levison to inspect. The chain slid back and the door opened.

"It's very late but please come in."

He followed the doctor into the living room and Levison muted the television. The remains of a T.V. dinner sat on the arm of a chair and a crystal glass of an amber liquid sat next to a half-drunk bottle of Scotch whiskey.

"Please, take a seat," Levison said.

Monroe smiled and sat in a chair angled to the side of Levison's.

"I'm sorry to bother you at this time of night but I'm investigating a number of murders that may be connected to the killing of one of your own employees."

"Oh? I thought the M.O.D. police were dealing with that."

"Of course. That's right but they don't have jurisdiction over the murders in London."

"That's not what I was led to believe."

"I'm just trying to get my head around all this. I'd just like to have an idea of the work you are doing at the laboratory."

Levison sucked air through his teeth. "I'm afraid it's classified."

"I understand that," Monroe said, nodding, "I've signed the official secrets act and I only want an overview of the type of work you do, not specifics."

Levison picked up his whiskey and took a sip. "Would you like one?" he held up his glass.

"I've got the car."

He nodded. "All I can tell you is that I'm a geneticist. I have spent my life researching the question of 'nature or nurture.' Do you know what that means?"

"I think so," Monroe said. "It's whether a child becomes good or bad through being born like that or whether the environment plays a factor."

Levison smiled. "That's pretty much it, yes."

"So, what was Doctor Felicity Saunders' role at the lab?"

"I'm sure it's well documented in your files."

"Humour me, please," Monroe said.

Another sip of whiskey seemed necessary as Levison pondered his reply. "She was the lead scientist in the genetic research lab. She oversaw the process of extracting the D.N.A. from the samples we use in our research."

"The samples? Where do they come from?"

Levison looked uncomfortable. He knew he had overstepped the line in ordering Big Mike to sort out the snoopers, but he had not intended for anyone to get hurt.

"Look, I'm leaving tomorrow. I've got to get away. I'm caught up in something I have no control over and it's getting out of hand."

"What do you mean?"

Levison necked his drink and poured another. "It's a fucking mess," he said. "I was doing vital work, we all were. Then, about twenty years ago, we were running out of funding and a colleague in my old university suggested I speak to this financier from New York. He said the man was keen to invest in genetic technology. He had some crazy idea we could create a new generation of children that would be the best of all we could be. I thought he was mad, but the man was a billionaire and keen to part with his money."

"Go on."

"I never met him, nor did I speak to him directly. The colleague at Cambridge organised everything there was no real paperwork and that triggered an alarm for me but, stupidly, I chose to ignore it. I either accepted the money or the whole project would come crashing down. What harm would it do? I thought. I'd go through the motions and then report back that genetic engineering of people was not possible."

"Fraud?"

Levison blushed. "I was desperate."

"OK."

"Well, the truth is, the engineering is not just possible... it's been done."

"What?"

"Cloning, it's been done."

Monroe couldn't believe what he was hearing. "But that's outlawed by all governments..."

Levison laughed nervously. "They're all doing it. The U.S.A., Britain, Russia, and just about every developed country in the world are trying to develop the perfect specimen," he said with a sneer. "We were bankrolled by the financier and then the government. Our government found out and rather than shut us down they got some clandestine group within the M.O.D. to oversee our work. They had recognised the potential for military use. It became a bloody nightmare."

"This is unbelievable."

"But true, nonetheless. We use volunteers and samples of D.N.A. that are sourced by our partners."

"Your partners?"

"As I said, the American financier and we are overseen by a government department so, as you can imagine, we have to be stringent in the recording of our work. When this all got out of hand, I realised the recording was my only chance to escape. I copied the sensitive files and I have them hidden."

"Can I see them?"

He shook his head. "They are my safety net. I'm sorry but I'm risking my life talking to you like this."

"What about copies, could I have copies or perhaps a sample?"

He thought about it for a moment. "That might be possible."

"OK, so tell me the rest."

"As I said, we had to account for everything we did. Felicity was brilliant, quite, quite brilliant. There was nothing she didn't know. She excelled at the management of projects due to her thorough understanding of each and every process."

"You mentioned volunteers. What are they used for?"

"It's mainly for confirming research that has already been carried out in the past to establish a baseline from which we can then take things further. That part of our work is restricted but I can tell you the earlier stuff. Basically, we were just monitoring the personality and other traits of the volunteers compared to the traits exhibited by their genetic parents and, in the case of adopted volunteers, how they compare to their adoptive parents. That gives us a picture of how the genes determine these outcomes. It's good evidence but not entirely empirical, so that's what we are trying to pin down definitively."

Monroe nodded. "Interesting."

"I think so, yes. But we were having pressure applied to take chances, to push the boundaries."

"The cloning?"

"Exactly."

"Did Felicity ever mention anything in this work of hers or perhaps her private life that might have been a motive for her murder?"

"Everything we all did was motive for murder," Levison scoffed.

"Perhaps, but someone had a specific reason to kill her and I'd be grateful for anything that could help me find her killer."

"As I said, the M.O.D. are dealing with her death and I'm afraid I'm not a party to their enquiry. I'm not sure they really want to find out because they're part of the whole mess."

"I understand that, but if I can find a motive for her death then it might help with the others that aren't within the M.O.D. remit."

"Why don't you speak with their investigators?"

It was a good question, but Monroe had already tried that route of enquiry and to date he was still waiting for a reply. "Let's just say that the M.O.D. aren't exactly forthcoming with information, and what you told me would make sense. I'm afraid if they don't share what they have we could potentially miss links that connect Felicity to the other murders."

"You think they're connected? I don't see how. I said we all had reason to be silenced but Felicity didn't have any specific information that would make her stand out. I knew more, which is why I'm getting out."

"I'd strongly advise you to stay and give evidence. You're up to your neck in this."

"I was acting on orders. I never wanted anyone hurt. It wasn't until I discovered the source of D.N.A. of the Whitechapel File that I began to panic."

"The Whitechapel File?"

"All the projects had sub-~~projects,~~ projects; they were hidden within the uncontentious parts of the research. The Whitechapel D.N.A. was taken from something ~~stolen from~~ our benefactor had. Seems he was also a wealthy collector of unique objects."

Monroe shrugged his shoulders and frowned as he thought about the killings. The only connection he could find at present was that all the intended victims were female. He agreed with Wise about the poor vagrant. The chap probably just disturbed the killer and was collateral damage. But what if the man was also an intended target? Wise had taught Monroe to never discount any possibility. "Whitechapel was the location of a series of murders in the nineteenth century," he finally said.

Levison nodded.

Sitting in his car outside Levison's home, Monroe checked his phone signal. Four G in the capital was good and he quickly scrolled through Google for a search terms he had tapped in; 'Nature versus Nurture.' There was a lot of research already available, some dating back to the seventies and most of it suggested that when twins were for some reason or other separated at birth and then reunited later in life, they invariably displayed remarkably similar personality traits. These traits extended to likes and dislikes, whether they were smokers, gay or straight and even included their acceptance of religion. [1] There were dozens of reports to read and Monroe had no intention of reading any of them in the car. He scrolled through the author names

---

[1] https://www.livescience.com/47288-twin-study-importance-of-genetics.html

for the research papers and none of them seemed to be attributed to Felicity. Perhaps her research hadn't been released to the public domain just yet – it was obviously classified, as Levison suggested. If a private company was sponsoring the research and had profits to consider then it would make sense, but was the government interested in those commercial considerations too? Knowing the British Government, Monroe guessed the commercial implications of any research that promised some kind of fiscal reward would not be ignored. But what the hell could this kind of research achieve for them? Everyone knew cloning humans was a no-go area for research.

There was plenty of research out there already, Google attested to that, but it didn't make sense. This lab was behind the murders, but the link between the victims couldn't be established. Perhaps there was no link? Perhaps the lab had tried to create a perfect example of humanity and ended up with a monster, something like Mary Shelley's Frankenstein? More likely was the need to keep the research out of the public domain. The cloning of humans would cause a stink that would have far reaching consequences for the government and anyone involved and that was enough reason for them to kill to keep it quiet. Monroe had no proof to justify spending hours going through the existing research without the files

Levison said he had. The scientist promised to email a copy of some of the files and Monroe had warned him to stay safe and not to leave the country. Had he not been warned off the case he would have taken Levison in for questioning further, under caution, but he had overstepped the mark already and would probably lose his job and his pension.

    He started his engine and pulled off into the evening traffic. A light rain had begun to spot the windscreen as he scrolled through the radio for a channel playing classical music. He wasn't a particular fan of the music, but he always found it helped him to think. It was probably because most of it didn't have lyrics. Lyrics always seemed to worm their way in to his head and disrupt his train of thought. Even better was the programme was playing a selection of movie themes from John Williams, not what Monroe thought was true classical music, but it seemed to fit into the modern genre that he particularly loved.

    The theme from Jurassic Park began to play and Monroe wondered if it was a sign. The film was about genetic engineering. There had been outrage at the research into genetically altered crops, so it would make sense. No government would want to divulge their involvement in anything that could be loading bullets in the guns of religious fundamentalists. Perhaps that was it. Perhaps Felicity had gone to the press about the work there and someone wanted her stopped. But then how did the other victims fit into the picture? They didn't fit, not in any way that he could think of.

He used his hands-free set to call a contact at the M.O.D. When the M.O.D. took over the investigation into the killing of Doctor Felicity, Monroe had been surprised to see the name of the Ministry man in charge. Padraig Collins was the name of a young man who had joined the Met with Monroe decades ago. There couldn't be many with that name, he thought. But if it was the same man then why was he with the M.O.D.? The last Monroe had heard of him was that he had been required to resign from the Met for his involvement in allegedly fitting up a suspect in an armed robbery case whilst he was with the Flying Squad.

He spoke to his contact and asked for background on Collins. Satisfied that it was the same man, he asked for his mobile number.

## CHAPTER 31

The man called Collins stood in the doorway of a card shop that had been closed for more than four hours. It was a strange place to meet but at least it wasn't the stereotypical park bench.

Monroe stood on the pavement, so the man was technically trapped in the doorway, not a wise choice of meeting place for him. He did, however, look like he could take care of himself. He was taller than Monroe, perhaps six-two, and weighed average for that height, but his jaw was square, and looked like it could take the blow of a sledgehammer. His hair was difficult to see in the dark and under the black beanie hat he wore but Monroe thought there was a hint of ginger in the man's eyebrows.

"Thanks for coming," Monroe said.

Collins lit a cigarette and blew the smoke towards Monroe. "Would you like one?"

"I gave up years ago, but I could really do with a smoke right now. The man tapped another from his pack and handed it to him. Monroe nodded a thanks and let the man light the end for him.

"I'm taking a risk here, you know that, right? Collins said.

"I'm not going to say anything to anyone, not yet anyway."

"Not at all, not what I tell you."

"~~Okay~~OK. Nice to see you again," Monroe said with a smile. "I thought you resigned?"

"I did. Didn't have a choice. I was stitched up. Anyway, that's not what this is about." Collins took another long drag, his face glowing in the red flare from his cigarette. "You know I don't owe you anything? It's not like we kept in touch or were ever best buddies."

"This isn't about friendship, this is about what's right and what's wrong."

Collins snorted and smiled. "OK. It's like you thought. It's all down to the lab."

"Didn't take a brain surgeon to guess that one."

"But you'll never get the inside info. The file of Doctor Felicity's murder has been sealed tighter than a nun's knickers."

"Why?"

Another two drags of the smoke before Collins spoke again. "Because the lab is not just government funded but government run. The whole fucking project is set up and operated through a proxy company that's answering directly to H.M.~~GMG~~. A well-known American billionaire is putting huge sums of money into the project."

"You mean the government is running a false company to hide its own involvement?"

"Exactly. And the files relating to the research are shocking to read."

"I understand it's all to do with nature and nurture, how kids want to play and behave when born the same... like twins, but separated... genetics and shit like that?"

He nodded. "That might well be the case but from the briefing I received from Levison when we were first assigned the case, I think it's more Jurassic Park than Brockwell Park."

Monroe coughed as he took a lungful of smoke. "He has a file he said he'll email to me. He also said they had been cloning humans?"

"They're officially just observing genetic differences, but they're not just observing the differences... they're creating them."

\*\*\*

The email hadn't arrived. Monroe cursed. Levison swore he'd get it to him before midnight, but nothing had come through.

Monroe rang the mobile number Levison had given him and the call went straight to answerphone.

There was nothing for it, he'd have to go back and drag the bastard out of his house and down to the nick. He felt guilty for not doing it the first time around. He was a copper, a bloody senior detective and he hadn't done his job.

It took him under twenty minutes to get back to Levison's home. He knocked the door and waited. The lights were still on in the living room.

Monroe walked to the front window and peered in through the cracks in the blinds. There was no sign of Levison.

He tried the door handle and the door opened. Monroe called out, "Doctor Levison?"

He checked the downstairs rooms and then climbed the stairs to the bedrooms. Clothes were strewn across the bed and the wardrobe door was open. Levison had gone. The bastard had taken off.

\*\*\*

The night was special for Wise. It had been a long time since he had been so close to a woman, especially one as attractive as Sam. He had long ago accepted that such nights would no longer be his. Sam had changed that mindset overnight, now he truly believed there was a possibility that he could find love again. Sam had given him hope. Something as simple as a night of passion had restored his spirit.

He made a pot of coffee as Sam slept. It was still early but Sam had told him she needed to be up before five to open the café for the breakfasts.

He kissed her lightly on her forehead as he placed the mug on the bedside table. Sam's eyes fluttered open and she smiled. "That's smells good," she yawned.

"Thought you deserved a treat after last night, something to replenish your energy."

She giggled. "Take more than coffee to do that. You've worn me out."

"Excuse me," Wise snorted. "I think it was you that wore me out." They both laughed.

Sam sat up in bed and the duvet dropped to reveal part of her burn. She hurriedly covered it again, but Wise stopped her. He pulled the cover down and kissed the scar.

She sighed. "Do you know how much that means to me?"

"I can guess," he said honestly. "Do you know how much this all means to me?"

She nodded and shrugged. "We've both got damaged packaging but that doesn't mean the goods inside should be returned for a refund."

"I was beginning to think my damage had affected the inside too. I've spent too long feeling sorry for myself."

"Well, today is the start of a new life. I'd like to see you again if you would too."

He kissed her full on the lips and held her tight. "There's nothing I'd like more. But I have to sort this mess out first."

"You know where I am. Just give me a call."

Sam got out of bed and carried her coffee into the bathroom. He heard the shower run and walked into the kitchen. He pushed four pieces of bread into the toaster.

After breakfast, Sam kissed him and left for work. Wise promised her he would call her as soon as he cleared his name. The last thing he wanted was to get her involved any more than she already was.

\*\*\*

Godfrey and Doug stood in the shadows of a corner of the subterranean car park. They had been there for over an hour and had stayed hidden as residents had collected their cars and motorcycles for the day.

Doug nudged Godfrey when the lift door opened and a woman walked out carrying a crash helmet.

"He must be still in the flat," Godfrey said. "She'll have the key."

They ran silently across the car park and Doug grabbed Sam as she sat on the moped. He pulled her off the bike and both bike and Sam toppled onto the ground. Doug held her by the throat as Godfrey took the keys from the ignition. Sam struggled against the big man but the more she struggled the tighter his grip became. She couldn't breath and her head felt like it would explode.

Doug looked to Godfrey for directions; Doug did nothing without his friend's instructions. "We don't want her and can't let her identify us." That was all Doug needed. He squeezed her neck until she fell still.

\*\*\*

The key needed changing. He heard it rattle in the lock. Wise promised himself that he would sort it out for Sam next time he visited her. She must have forgotten something. He smiled as the door opened but the smile quickly slipped from his face. Two men stood in the doorway. It was the two thugs that had been in the van and had been responsible for the murder of the old woman. The smaller of the two stood in front of the other. The big black guy looked like a professional wrestler. The little guy just looked mean.

How did they have Sam's key? A feeling of dread washed over Wise. "Where's Sam?"

The little guy sneered. "Was that her name? Pretty woman, wasn't she? I don't think her end was painless, but it was quick. Quicker than it would have been had a friend of ours got hold of her. So, you could say we did her a favour. Can't say we'll afford the same courtesy to you," he said calmly.

Now the dread had turned to anger, a rapidly rising rage unlike anything Wise had felt before. Even in his darkest days he had never allowed himself to succumb to the feelings he knew would destroy him. It had been a hard battle, one that had progressively got harder as time passed and his life seemed destined for solitude. Sam had changed that but now that hope had been cruelly dashed. Wise saw a kitchen bread knife on the counter to his right. It was long and sharp, and he had used it less than half an hour ago to make the breakfast. Now he'd use it to for something far more sinister. He snatched it and ran at the little man. He ducked and rammed his head into the man's face. He heard the cracking of bone as the little man fell back into the man mountain behind him. Both fell back through the open door and into the hallway. The big guy roared and threw his little friend from him. As he struggled to find his feet, Wise kicked him in the face. The big man's nose burst across his left cheek, but he kept on coming. Wise punched out with his left fist, a long by quick jab that caught the big man's mangled nose. He grunted in pain but staggered towards Wise. Wise saw his chance and thrust the blade deep into the big man's heart. The man collapsed to the tiled floor and blood pumped from the wound as Wise pulled the blade free.

The little guy was semi-conscious, holding his face and rolling on the hall floor. Wise stepped over the big man and grabbed the little guy by the hair. He pulled him up against the wall and banged the knife down into the top of his head. The crunch of bone as the knife pierced the scull and the little guy's brain was strangely satisfying. Wise felt no guilt, no remorse. The bastards both deserved to die.

Wise left the knife embedded in the man's head. He made no attempt to wipe his prints from the handle, what was the point? His hope for a new life had ended there in that doorway and he would gladly accept whatever fate was now in store for him.

He ignored the lift and took the emergency stairwell to the car park. He saw Sam lying next to her moped, her helmet some feet away from her prone body. He ran to her but knew he was too late. He checked her pulse and her eyes opened. She coughed and Wise began to cry. The sense of relief was like someone had pulled a plug out of him and let the angry air hiss out. He bent over her and kissed her, brushed loose hair from her face and smiled. Once more he felt the guilt that seemed to follow and haunt him all the days of his life. Someone had put a contract out on Wise and Sam had almost been killed, like the old woman and now Martine was in hospital. Someone had to pay. He helped Sam into the lift, and they rode to her floor. She gasped at the sight of the two men lying in her doorway, but Wise manoeuvred her around the bodies and into the flat. He sat her on the settee and told her to wait for a moment. He had to get the bodies away from her flat, somewhere they wouldn't be associated with her. Perhaps they had already been discovered and perhaps the police were already on their way, but he had to do something. He lifted the big guy under his arms and dragged him along the corridor to the stairwell where he pushed him through the fire door and down the stairs. He ran back to the thin man and this time it was easier to carry him to the same stairs and push him down on top of his dead friend.

    Returning to the flat, he removed the key from the outside lock of Sam's door, rushed to the cupboard where she kept a bucket and mop and quickly mopped up the blood in the doorway. Satisfied, he shut the door behind him. Sam was staring at him in shock.

"I'm so sorry," he said.

Sam shook her head. "They caught me by surprise. I didn't hear them coming."

"Are you OK?"

She nodded. "I think so, my throat is sore, the bastard tried to choke me to death."

Wise sat next to her and held her in his arms. "I'm so sorry. I thought I'd lost you. It's all my fault."

She went stiff. "How did they die? Did you kill them?"

Wise broke the embrace, stood and walked to the window. "They said you were dead and I…" he left the words unsaid. Sam stood and walked towards him. She turned him to face her. "You did that for me?"

"I… I just lost it. You were just helping me and then they…"

She held his head and pulled him to her. She kissed him hard on the mouth then buried her head in his shoulder. "What are we going to do now? The police will charge you with murder."

"I'll think of something," Wise said with more conviction than he truly held.

They sat together for a while, saying nothing more, each deep in thought. He needed to check on Martine and reluctantly stood to leave. "Are you going to be OK? You need to come with me. I have to check on my sister. I don't think those bastards have anyone else working with them, but I'd feel better if you're near me."

Sam smiled and nodded. "I'll be fine."

They took the lift back to the car park and lifted Sam's moped back up onto the stand. The last thing he wanted was for some clever copper to connect the toppled bike to two murdered men in the stairwell. It would only be a matter of time before the local uniforms were swarming all over the building and they would want to interview everyone in the building.

They walked to the first twenty-four-hour store and bought another burner phone. He popped the sim card into the device and called Monroe.

"I'll be at the hospital at nine..."

Wise interrupted, "There's been another attack. A friend of mine. She was helping me. The same two thugs almost choked her to death."

"Jesus! Where?"

"In the basement car park of her apartment. You'll hear the calls soon."

"OK, I'm sorry, mate."

"There's more," Wise continued. "I killed them both. They're lying in the stairwell of Sam's apartment."

"This is a fucking nightmare," Monroe gasped.

## CHAPTER 32

Tina Thompson felt like a little girl waiting for Santa Claus to arrive with presents on Christmas day. Isaac was late. He promised to log on at the same time each night, but he'd missed two nights now and she was wondering if he had lost interest. Her excitement peaked again when she saw a green light appear next to his cartoon image on the dating site.

"Hi babe," he said as the facetime app opened.

"Hi," she beamed back. "You look hot."

"So do you," he said.

Isaac stood naked before the camera, his erect manhood sending remote shivers up Tina's spine.

"You still on for tonight?" she asked.

"What do you think?" he grinned back

~~Tine~~ Tina lifted her black silk top to reveal her large, firm breasts. "Can't wait for you to play with my puppies," she teased.

"Your puppies can play hide my sausage."

"Can't wait," she laughed.

Isaac clicked off the app and wrapped a towel around his waist. The woman was eager and had no idea what she was arranging. Things were progressing well, but Wise was still free and would no doubt be desperate to clear his name. There was only one way for Isaac to complete his plan. He had to point the finger of suspicion at someone else and he had already put the pieces in place. He honestly thought the patsy would have been picked up by now but the police had been disappointing. Wise was no longer a detective and the idiots running the investigation clearly needed a bigger hint. He had an idea. He donned a pair of rubber gloves and printed some images on paper taken from a sealed pack. He slipped them inside an envelope he had not touched with bare fingers and didn't bother sealing it. If this didn't get them looking where he wanted, then there was no hope for the people of London. He smiled at the thought of them arresting the wrong man whilst he made his escape. It was time to move on. Europe was a possibility and so too was America. There were loads of serial killers and nutters in America. He laughed at the thought and headed for his wardrobe.

## CHAPTER 33

Sergeant Ted Angel knocked on the glass panel in acting Detective Chief Inspector Rickett's door. The door was a remnant of the past. Warped, aged and scarred by years of use and abuse, it was an echo from a time when it was acceptable and often expected to smoke in the hectic confines of the C.I.D. office. Painted white at some distant time, the smoke of a thousand or more cigarettes had discoloured it to an amber tone. The obscured glass pane rattled in its frame and Rickett shouted, "Enter."

The D.C.I.'s office was no more than ten feet square with one wall of metal filing cabinets to the right of the door. On the opposite wall was a shelving system that contained volumes of police procedures and updated criminal law and some personal framed mementoes of Rickett's service. One frame contained a dozen cap badges form various UK forces, another held shoulder patches from colleagues in other parts of the world. A class photo of Rickett's time at Hendon stood propped against the wall on one shelf and two smaller photos showed a beaming Rickett in uniform as a sergeant and recently promoted inspector. Rickett's desk was old and had probably been in the office for as long as the door had been in place. Dark oak and the size of a family dining table from the sixties, the desk looked like it could withstand a nuclear war. Rickett sat with his back to a window that overlooked the rear yard. He leaned back in his high back chair and tossed a black Biro onto the desk. "Ah, Ted. I wanted to speak to you. I need you to rotate the watch on Wise's sister at the hospital. I know it's not on our patch, but I want you to make sure the local boys don't fuck it up."

Ted nodded. "No worries. I'll give them a ring and warn them."

"They're holding her on suspicion of theft of a B.M.W. and Wise was with her when the car was crashed. He's still out there somewhere and he's bound to want to check on her."

Ted nodded again Rickett and held out a large brown envelope.

"What have you got, Ted?"

"Dropped into the front office by a guy in a hoodie earlier. I think you need to check out the contents."

Rickett took the envelope and pulled out three A4 photocopies of still images that were clearly taken from C.C.T.V. cameras. "What the hell is this?"

"Take a closer look," said the sergeant.

He held the photos closer to his face and then made the connection. "These are photos of the victims of the killer," he did a double take and sat forward, "and this is the same man with all three," he said as he tapped one of the photos.

"I think our mystery postman has dropped us our first piece of solid evidence, guv."

"Sure looks that way," Rickett agreed. "At least we can now point to the same man being present with each woman on the night of their deaths. It's got to be him."

"Look at the back."

Rickett flicked one of the photos over. On the back was a name and an address.

"We need to find whoever sent this. This bloke would be a great witness."

"Do you think it's genuine?"

"Probably someone who feels guilty. Wants to set the record straight and get this fucking idiot off the streets. Let's get the team together and organise a raid."

## CHAPTER 34

The call from Wise was short and just long enough to confirm that the ward was now clear. Monroe had shown the uniform constable his warrant card and told him to go and have a lunch break while he interviewed the woman under arrest. The constable was happy to oblige, and Wise had arrived within five minutes of him leaving. He walked into the ward wearing the white coat of a doctor.

"Where did you get that?"

"Security isn't what it should be," Wise said.

"You ~~okay~~OK?"

"As good as anyone can be when they've been framed for murder, their sister's in hospital and a woman who helped him was nearly killed and he's now also a killer. So, yeah. I'm just peachy."

"What about the woman, is she ~~okay~~OK?"

"She's in the café downstairs, waiting."

Monroe's phone vibrated in his jacket pocket again and he held up his hand. "Got to take this," he said and stepped out of the ward.

Wise sat on the end of Martine's bed. She was fast asleep, and he didn't want to disturb her. Her head injury was diagnosed as a concussion and she'd need to rest.

Four beds with four patients occupied the small ward, painted white, the ceiling tiles were some equally white insulation material that were held in place by a chessboard of aluminium frames. Two of the beds opposite Martine were enclosed by the drapes that hung on more aluminium frames.

Monroe walked back in with a smile on his face. "Got news. I think we have our killer."

Ted Angel had made the call to Monroe. The two men had been friends for many years but Ted's loyalty to Monroe exceeded just friendship. Ted had been the station sergeant for several years after he had been assaulted on duty. The attack had left him with a metal plate inserted in his skull and Monroe had pulled out all the stops to bring his assailant to justice. Ted had received a small amount of compensation from the Criminal Injuries Compensation Board, not enough to retire but enough to make his life a little easier and he had been grateful to Monroe for his help. It was that loyalty that had made him risk his career to call Monroe and update him with the news of the suspect he had revealed to Rickett.

"Ted just called. It seems some anonymous member of the public has just delivered photos of the killer and was kind enough to supply a name and address for the twat too."

Wise stood and walked to the door. I'm going to wait in the car park. There's nothing I can do here. We need to get to the suspect's address before the local officers."

"I'll go get the constable to come back and follow you out. We'll take my pool car."

They collected Sam from the café, and drove out of the hospital and headed for Golders Green. It took them fifteen minutes to get there. There was no sign of any local officers yet.

The address Monroe had been given was an impressive looking Edwardian building in a tree lined street. The house was detached and a red brick, bay front building over three floors. The gable roof looked new, the tiles were red and a brighter colour than those either side of it.

Monroe parked the car in the only available space between two of the Maple trees. Sam promised to stay in the car with the doors locked and they walked fifty metres back to the address.

Wise opened the front gate and walked down the side of the house to the back while Monroe knocked the front door. It was all done without speaking, they both knew the routine when calling at a suspect's house. Someone always had to cover the back in case the suspect made a run for it out the back door.

The rear garden was compact but well laid out. A small square of a lawn was offset to the right with a path winding from the house, through established borders to a small wooden gate set in a high brick wall the colour of the house. Wise could see a line of broken glass cemented into the top of the wall to prevent unwelcome visitors.

There was no sign of life at the front. Monroe knocked several times before giving up and walking around to the rear. "No one home," he said.

Wise peered in through the glass pane in the back door. The kitchen was huge, bigger than his flat, well-appointed with white shiny kitchen units and black stone tops. It was equipped with every conceivable appliance and some Wise couldn't even imagine. The owner was certainly not short of a bob or two and that wasn't surprising. Monroe had told him that Ted had done a check on the suspect and he came back as a city banker with no criminal record. The man's name was Isaac Nicholls, aged thirty-nine. Born in North London to a single mother. Taken into foster care at the age of six months and had lived at a children's home from the age of four.

"We need to take a look around before the local boys and girls turn up," Wise said.

"We haven't got a warrant."

Wise grinned. "I think you need to check the front ~~again,~~ again; in case he comes home."

"You're not...? Shit!" Monroe shook his head and walked back along the path to the front.

A large rock formed a part of a small dry-stone wall bordering the lawn. Wise picked it up and smashed it against the pane of glass in the door. The glass shattered into millions of pieces and Wise tutted when he noticed the backdoor key had been left in the lock. He opened it and let himself inside. He could hear the alarm bleeping, warning the owner that it was about to activate. Wise followed the sound to a cupboard under the stair and tutted again when he saw four numbers written on the alarm box. He tapped them in on the pad and the alarm fell silent. "Bloody idiot," he muttered under his breath.

The hallway was grand. A glass multi-faceted chandelier hung by a chain from a high ceiling. A door to his left opened into a sitting room that was equally grand and expensively decorated. The largest flat screen television he had ever seen was mounted on the wall above a period fireplace. Two red Chesterfield settees were surrounded by antique ~~bookshelf~~ bookshelves that were crammed full of leather-bound volumes. Wise took the stairs to the first floor where three bedrooms were immaculately presented like images from a fancy magazine. Another staircase led to the top floor where another bedroom was empty. Another door was closed with a small enamelled sign that had two black letters; W.C. Wise opened the door and froze. The bath was full of water and a naked man was lying in it up to his chin. He hurried to the figure and checked his pulse. He was still breathing, though it was weak, and his skin had the pallor of death. Wise manhandled him over the side of the bath and the unconscious figure flopped onto the floor like a heavy, slippery trout. An empty bottle of tranquilisers lay next to the bath.

Wise placed the man in the recovery position and covered him with a bath towel before he ran down the stairs and let Monroe in through the front door.

"Our man has seemingly had a twinge of guilt and tried to top himself. He's taken tablets and nearly drowned in the bath."

"Shit! Where is he?"

Wise ran up the stairs, followed by Monroe. The man looked like the description Ted had given him. "Looks half dead."

"I think we need to get out of here before the local lads arrive."

"What if he recovers and runs off?"

"Does he look like it?"

"Who knows, are you a fucking doctor?"

Wise shook his head and took a wash towel to cover his hands as he rifled through bathroom cabinets affixed to the wall. He found what he was looking for – a roll of bandage. He unrolled it and tied it around the man's hands and then tying the other end to the radiator. "That'll hold him."

"And now they'll know someone has been here before them."

"Who gives a fuck? Come on, let's go."

They were driving out of one end of the road when a marked police car turned onto the road from the other end.

"That was close," Monroe said.

"I'm hungry," Wise said.

"~~Okay~~OK. Let's get something on our way to my place. You'll both have to stay with me."

"We can't do that. You'll lose your job. You can't do that."

"You've got nowhere else to go."

Monroe was right. Wise had no family or friends he could call, and they couldn't return to Sam's flat. "I think better after some food."

They turned into a McDonald's drive through and joined a line of vehicles ordering through a remote system. They waited until they had ordered their food before Monroe began to tell Wise of his meeting with Collins from the M.O.D.

"It seems that the lab is using some guise of social research to cover their real interest which is genetics."

"Explain, I don't understand."

"This Collins fella said the M.O.D. investigation has been hampered too but that what he was able to find out was that some government department is financing the research. It's true that there is one area of the lab that is carrying out research into D.N.A. and another part of it is doing studies into the question of nature or nurture, you know, whether we are born with certain immutable traits or whether we develop traits as a result of our environment."

Sam leaned forward, her head between the front seats, intently listening.

Wise nodded. "OK."

"But there seems to be a top-secret cross-over between these two groups. From what I understand, it looks like they are also taking what they learn and are applying it in genetic experiments. I even found out that they aren't just using D.N.A. from volunteers, they have been harvesting whatever they can get from the exhibits stored in old murder cases."

"What?"

"It's true, I verified it for myself."

"What cases are we talking about and how does this all make sense?"

"I checked some old cases and one in particular made a scary connection."

Now Wise was very interested. "Go on," he said.

"Well, I'm not saying this is possible or even sane but one of the cases they have accessed and extracted D.N.A. is from the Whitechapel Murders… there was just a single item kept from the old Jack the Ripper killings. It was the Eddowes shawl and it was bought by a collector who had it stolen over thirty years ago. It's rumoured to have been stolen by an unknown wealthy American financier and then shipped to the U.K. for this crackpot plan."

Sam slumped back in her seat. "You must be fucking kidding."

## CHAPTER 35

"Who the hell beat us to it and how the fuck did they know?" Rickett raged.

"Does it matter now, guv? At least we have the bastard. I'd guess it was the guy who gave us the tip-off," Detective Constable Kirsty Slade said. Slade had worked with Monroe for nearly two years and wasn't happy that she now had to work for Rickett. It wasn't that Rickett was a bad copper, it was just that he could be a bit of a wanker, difficult at best.

Slade wiped her long brown hair from her face and took a scrunchie from her pocket to tie it back in a bun. Satisfied, she stepped into the bathroom and grinned at the sight of the naked man tied to the radiator. "Big boy," she chuckled.

"I'd remind you I expect only complete professionalism at all times, D.C. Slade."

"Sorry, sir," Slade said in mock deference.

"Let's get the bastard checked out by the quack and into an interview room. I want him more than anything I've ever wanted."

"Oh, sir," Kirsty mumbled quietly so Rickett couldn't hear her.

It was nearly four hours later that the suspect was deemed fit enough to be interviewed. He had recovered quickly and swore he hadn't taken any of the tranquilisers. He told the charge room sergeant that he had only drunk a glass of orange juice before he went in the bath and didn't remember anything after that until he woke up in the ambulance. His recovery had been quicker than the doctors at the hospital had seen from an overdose, and bloods and other tests revealed nothing abnormal. The hospital had wanted to keep him in for observations, but Isaac had signed a release paper and volunteered to be interviewed. The force doctor also checked him over when he got to the station and both he and the solicitor were happy for the interview to go ahead.

Rickett assembled his team of detectives in the C.I.D. office and ran through the evidence they had. He made it clear that he would interview Isaac and that he wanted Kirsty to sit in on the interview. He seemed to think that the presence of a woman might unsettle the suspect. Then he went through the questions that needed to be asked and the answered he wanted to get. He believed in having everything covered before ~~entering~~ starting the interview. Failing to plan was planning to fail and Rickett saw this case as his opportunity to take another step up the promotion ladder. He had been involved in a dozen or so murders during his time on the department, with different levels of responsibility as he progressed up through the ranks. This was a very different proposition. This was a serial killer he had in the station and he had to get it right.

Isaac sat in an interview room, dressed in a white paper coverall handed to him on arrival. The officers at his house were checking through everything and that included his clothes.

The room was small and the table was bolted to the floor. The chairs Isaac and the duty solicitor were sitting on were also bolted to the floor. He had spent nearly thirty minutes taking instructions from his client and had a note pad open on his desk with notes he had taken.

Rickett was keen to get the interview started and Kirsty explained the recording system that would be used to document the interview. Isaac was cautioned again and Rickett began.

"You have been arrested and cautioned on suspicion of murder." He read out the names of the victims, the times and the dates of each and then waited for a reply.

Isaac looked genuinely shocked. "I'm totally innocent," he said. "I don't know any of these people other than what I've seen on the news. You can't think I'd do anything like that. I wouldn't, couldn't hurt a fly."

Rickett crossed his arms. "We have photographs of you in the company of all the victims."

Kirsty opened a brown Manilla folder and spread the images out on the table. Isaac leaned forward and his eyes bulged in shock. "That's not me, that can't be me. I don't even know where these places are."

"Look at them again," Ricketts said. "Who does that look like?"

Isaac spluttered, "OK, I admit it looks like me but it can't be."

Rickett's nodded to Kirsty and she reached for a remote control. A flat screen television on the wall clicked on and she pressed another button. A video version of one of the stills flickered and began to play.

"We managed to get this footage off one of the CCTV's at a nightclub. Just watch," Rickett said.

They all watched the clip that lasted nearly ten minutes. It showed Isaac walking through a crowd at the club and sitting at the bar. He then began to talk to her a woman, but the video was silent. At the end, Kirsty pressed pause.

"So, what have you got to say to that?" Kirsty said.

Isaac sat back in his chair and shook his head. "Play it again. Did you notice the limp? The man was limping. I don't have a limp."

They replayed the recording and the limp was indeed evident. "Perhaps you twisted your ankle, perhaps it's better now?" Rickett suggested.

"I've got people who can vouch for me on those dates and none of them will say they saw me limping because I haven't had a limp since I got kicked in the ankle when I played football and I haven't played for nearly ten years. You've got the wrong man. This is someone who looks like me."

Rickett laughed. "Are you seriously saying this is some kind of doppelganger or a twin or something?"

Isaac looked to his solicitor and then back to Rickett. He clearly wanted to say something but wasn't sure he should.

"What?" Rickett said impatiently.

"I know this sounds crazy," Isaac said, "but it's just as crazy for me too."

"What?" Rickett said again.

"I was born a twin... but I was told my brother had died at birth. Several years ago, I wanted to find out what happened to him and contacted the adoption agency. They told me he had contracted meningitis as a little boy and had his foot amputated and then he died. I was brought up in a ~~home and had no family~~loving home, so never though much more about it."

Rickett looked at Kirsty and then back at Isaac. "~~You're~~ Are you shitting me?"

## CHAPTER 36

Carrying a tray of chocolate biscuits, Sergeant Ted Angel entered the C.I.D. office in the middle of a heated debate.

"It's him, I'm sure of it."

"What about the limp?" Kirsty asked Rickett as he paced the floor before the assembled detectives.

"It's bollocks. He probably twisted his ankle or pulled a fucking muscle and he's ~~okay~~ OK again now. He's had days to recover. He's lying. We need to get hold of his so-called witnesses and quash his alibi."

"I'll take Kirsty with me and do the lot today if we can," Detective Sergeant Ron ~~Bob~~ Toye said.

"Good," Rickett broke off when he saw Ted with the biscuits. "You diamond, Ted," he smiled.

The sergeant laid the tray on a desk next to a pot of coffee and a litre bottle of milk the team were helping themselves to. Ted poured himself a coffee in a plastic cup and moved away as the others did the same. He loitered at the back, listening to the frustrated conversations just long enough to pick up the information he needed then left.

A constable was walking in through the rear door to the station as Ted stepped out into the enclosed yard. He dialled Monroe's number and told him about Isaac and the man's defence that his twin might still be alive and that twin might be pretending to be Isaac.

*\*\*\**

They were sat in Monroe's house in Gore Road next to Victoria Park in South Hackney. The double-fronted terrace house was the only one amongst a dozen each side that was not shrouded in scaffolding and plastic sheets. Monroe had explained that the whole street was being renovated by landlords and private owners to make the most of the ever-increasing property prices. The yellow brick, three-storey house was modest in comparison to the one Isaac lived in in Golder's Green, but the front elevation faced the park and Wise reckoned it was still worth far more than he could afford. Monroe had parked his car in a garage at the bottom of the garden that was accessed by Morpeth Road.

Monroe excused himself as his phone began to play a jingle. "This might be interesting," he said as he opened a patio door out on to a wooden decked area at the rear.

"This is unbelievable," Sam said. "You can't really believe some nutter is out there thinking he's Jack the fucking Ripper?"

Wise shook his head. "I don't know what to believe. It's either someone who wants to be linked to the Ripper or... could D.N.A. and genetic research re-create Jack? That lab had apparently successfully cloned humans."

Sam laughed. "No way. Why the hell would they clone a serial killer? That's ridiculous. Remember the bloody fuss over Dolly the sheep? There's no way they could do that, they would never be allowed."

"The lab is government funded with the backing of some dodgy billionaire from the States. We all know the government does what it wants. I wouldn't put it past that shower of shit."

When Monroe returned, he looked confused. "That was my pal at the nick. He's just overheard Rickett talking to his team."

"And?" Wise said impatiently.

"And, it seems Isaac might not be the killer."

"What?"

"Isaac, the guy who was arrested, was a twin at ~~birth~~ and ~~that~~ the ~~twin~~ brother was believed to have died at birth. ~~Looks likeBut~~ did he; ~~didn't die andmaybe~~ he's out there, ~~might be out there~~ acting as his brother, Isaac, whilst he lives out his twisted fantasy."

"It seems obvious to me," Sam said.

Both men looked at her.

"If you've got a killer preying on women you need to set him up, dangle some bait and see if the bastard bites."

"What the hell are you suggesting?" Wise said.

"I'm a woman. I'm sure I could lure him if you get me somewhere he hunts."

Wise shook his head. "Apart from the fact that would be extremely dangerous, the chances of us having you in the right place at the right time is near impossible."

"I'm a big girl. It might take a few days but it's worth a try," Sam insisted.

"She might be right," Monroe said.

"No way. It's not going to happen," Wise snapped.

## CHAPTER 37

He knew he looked good. Caine~~Isaac~~ stared at himself in the mirror and winked at himself.

Dressed in a charcoal black suit over a white shirt left open at the neck, he donned his black leather boots and checked his prosthetic foot. The boot helped to minimise the limp, but it never disguised it all together.

A taxi took him from his home in Mile End to Whitechapel. It stopped outside the Barts and London School of Medicine where he had studied nearly fifteen years before ~~under a different name~~, a time that had shaped his life before the urge began. In truth, the urge had always been there, he felt like he had been born with it. The first time he allowed it to manifest itself was the day he graduated as a Doctor of Medicine. The night had been brilliant. Surrounded by his fellow students, he had got wasted on a cocktail of drink and drugs and, looking back at that night, he was sure his loss of faculties had flicked a switch inside him. He had awoken in a student's flat the next morning with woman lying in bed next to him. He had beaten her to death and had felt disgusted with himself. That was no way for a woman to die. He couldn't remember killing the girl and he could think of much better ways to end a life, and he was ashamed and furious that he had succumbed to the urge without experiencing the pleasure. He would still be<u>en</u> a practicing doctor now had he not be struck off the General Medical Register for his behaviour during <u>his</u> time at accident and emergency. His temper and erratic response to trauma victims had brought him to the attention of his supervisors and none of them had understood him. They said he had succumbed to a breakdown when he fondled a female patient in front of colleagues. He had become violent when admonished for something he saw as being a perk of the job and psychological and psychiatric assessments had labelled him in need of sectioning.

He paid the fare and left a ten-pound tip. He watched the taxi pull away before he doubled back and pushed through the door into The Good Samaritan public house.

Tina Thompson was already there. She sat in a corner of the bar with a pint of Guinness in her hand. She smiled when she saw Caine enter. She watched him walk up to the bar and order another Guinness and whiskey. He carried the drinks to her table and sat opposite her. "You look good," he said.

"Anything to make you horny, Isaac," she said.

<u>Caine</u>~~Isaac~~ laughed. It was handy having a twin, a twin who believed you were dead.

## CHAPTER 38

Dressed in a black leather skirt, cut just above her knees, and over black stockings and a black sheer blouse over a black bra, Sam walked into the club where the Ripper had picked up one of his first victims.

Her long blonde hair was loose and styled straight. She wore blood red lipstick and her eye makeup was slightly overdone. Wise thought she looked great, but Sam had said she felt like a tart. Monroe had said that the look was exactly what the killer would be looking for.

Wise had argued vehemently against Sam being used as bait, but Sam had been the force behind the decision.

Monroe and Wise had eventually agreed and used a map of the area to work out the possible predatory areas. The Ripper hadn't strayed far and Wise knew from experience that some killers like him liked to taunt the police by following a pattern.

Both Monroe and Wise used Monroe's warrant card to observe the interior of the club from the security office where three flat screen monitors were each split into four views from C.C.T.V. cameras throughout the building. The only areas not covered by the cameras were the toilets so Wise felt a little easier. He knew they could be anywhere in the club in less than a minute.

It was just after ten p.m. when Sam had entered the club and it was nearly two hours later that she was approached by a man at the bar. Wise and Monroe were on high alert, but he quickly moved off and he looked nothing like Isaac.

Were they really expecting the killer to just waltz into the club and home on Sam? It was very unlikely, but it was the only thing they could do.

No one approached her again and at two-thirty Monroe met her at the bar and escorted her out to the car where Wise was waiting.

Sam got into the back and Wise slid in alongside her. "So, I'm chauffeur now, eh?" Monroe said.

"Do you know some bloke asked me how much I charge," Sam said indignantly.

Wise chuckled. "Hope you told him he could never afford you?"

Sam laughed. "Oh, you are nice."

"But stupid. I should never have let you do that tonight. You could have…"

"Could have but wasn't." She kissed him and Wise hugged her close, relieved that she was safe and somehow strangely delighted that she had cared so much ~~aim~~ that she would put her own life on the line to help him out.

"You two love birds need to get a room," Monroe said. "We still have the little problem of a psycho running around."

They broke the hug and Sam put her hand on Monroe's shoulder. "Hang on, don't go yet. All that juice I've drunk needs to go before you pull off or you'll have a puddle in your police car."

Wise grinned. "Don't be long."

\*\*\*

Caine needed one last drink. It had been a wonderful night.

Tina had played her part so well. She had been eager to be alone and who was Caine to spoil her fun?

He had killed her in the hospital car park. It was the perfect end to his mission in London, another ticked off his 'to-do list.' It was time to move on, at least for a while, until things cooled down a bit. It was never wise to stay in the same place too long, and he had booked a ticket for the Eurostar for the following week. He thought about going immediately but that would spoil the fun. He wanted to read the newspaper report, see the television news presenters pretending to be horrified by the loss of another young woman and listen to the radio broadcasts doing the same. It would be a media fest for him and he also needed a few days to sort out his room at the ward. He would have to do things right. He had more freedom there than he deserved but that didn't mean he could just waltz onto a train for France without someone coming after him. He had to give himself time and he knew just how to do that. There were eight hours between shift changeovers, and he had no qualms about silencing the eight members of staff before leaving. He could do it within the first hour of their start and have seven hours before the bodies were discovered. It would be sweet.

He walked towards the nightclub. The place held good memories for him. He saw the blonde woman enter ahead of him. She looked sexy. He checked his watch, it was nearly two-thirty. She was certainly a rare one – going for drinks at that time of night. Others were leaving the club and hailing taxis for the journey home.

Caine walked in and smiled. The night was young and perhaps his fun wasn't over yet.

***

"She's some woman," Monroe said. "You look good together."

Wise smiled. "It's early days but she makes me feel… good, I suppose."

"Make the most of it. My mum always told me to make the most of every day. I just wish she had taken he own advice."

"Oh?"

"Spent her whole life looking after me and my dad and what did my dad do as way of thanks?"

Wise shrugged.

"Ran off with some woman young enough to be his daughter. Killed my mother. She was never the same again. Bastard."

"Sorry, I had no idea. You always seemed to be someone who had it all, you know?"

Monroe turned in his seat to look at Wise. "No, I don't. What do you mean?"

"I remember the first day you came onto the department as an aide. You were always confident. You seemed driven and keen. Sometimes too bloody keen." Both men laughed.

"I guess it was my mother's advice. I joined the job after bumming around as a shop assistant. I wanted to give the job a good go and I was determined to make the most of it."

"I had always wanted to be a copper. Never wanted to do anything else. Used to watch the Sweeney when I was a kid and though Regan and

Carter were the real superheroes, not fucking Batman and Superman. These two ordinary guys, with all their flaws, were out there on the streets bringing the bad guys to justice and that's what I wanted to do too."

"I was more into Postman Pat," Monroe said.

\*\*\*

The blonde looked sexy. She was just his type. He'd get chatting to her over a drink or two. It would be the perfect nightcap for the perfect evening. Caine followed her towards the toilets. He saw her enter. He waited a moment for a pair of drunken women to stagger out then slipped into the Ladies. The blonde had disappeared, but one cubicle was occupied. He pulled the scalpel from his jacket pocket and waited.

\*\*\*

Wise checked his watch. She was taking her time. "I'm going to check on her."

Monroe nodded. "Yeah. Perhaps we shouldn't have let her go on her own."

"Thanks, make me feel good, why don't you?"

Monroe laughed.

Wise walked past the doorman and nodded. The doorman nodded back.

The toilet door was closed and Wise knocked. "Sam, Sam, come on. We need to go."

Nothing.

He knocked again. Still nothing. Wise suddenly felt an icy grip on his heart. Something was wrong.

The door opened slowly, Wise was suddenly afraid of what he might find. His worst fears were instantly realised. A large pool of blood was seeping out under a cubicle door. He shook his head. This couldn't be happening, not now, not when things had changed for him, not to Sam. He walked in a trance-like state to the door and then began to wail. Sam's body had been brutalised, her stomach sliced open through her blouse and her throat had been cut. He knew he was too late to help her and the anger had burst through his system like a supercharged explosion of electricity. He punched the cubicle door and his fist went through the melamine panel.

He ran for the door, the killer had to be close. The doorman looked shocked at Wise's appearance. "Did a guy just walk out of here, a dark haired, good-looking man?"

The doorman pointed outside. "Just before you came in," he said.

\*\*\*

Caine had noticed the unmarked police car outside the club. He had stood in a doorway and wiped the blood from his hands as a man with a severely burnt face stepped from the car and headed for the club entrance. It was the ex-copper, Wise. No one else could be that fucking ugly, he thought to himself.

He walked to the police car. A man in a suit was behind the steering wheel, flicking though his mobile phone. He didn't look up until Caine tapped on the window. The man in the suit buzzed down the window and then froze. He had recognised him. Caine smiled then stabbed the man in his right eye, deep and with force. The man was dead before Caine pulled out the knife.

\*\*\*

Monroe was slumped over the wheel when Wise got back to the car. Wise wanted to scream at him, to tell him that Sam was dead, that his life was fucked again but Monroe wasn't listening, Monroe would never listen again. The blood was everywhere, even down the side of the driver's door.

There was no point, but he checked Monroe's pulse. Nothing. Then he saw his friend's phone lying in his bloodied lap. He picked it up. Monroe had been searching through his contacts. A name and address were visible. Doctor Levison. He was the key to all this. This was the man responsible for unleashing hell on London again and it was time he was brought to justice.

Wise pulled his dead friend from the driver's seat and laid him gently on the pavement. He heard a woman scream somewhere close by but paid no attention. He got behind the wheel. He could feel the blood on the wheel and the warmth of it soaking through his trousers. None of that mattered. It was time for it all to end.

He started the car and pulled out in front of a taxi. He ignored the abuse from the driver and headed for Levison's home. The bastard was going to pay.

## CHAPTER 39

It was a little past three-thirty in the morning when Wise pulled up in Levison's street. There was nowhere to park, all the resident parking spaces occupied for the night, so he abandoned the car alongside a Mercedes SUV outside Levison's address.

Monroe had said Levison had flown the coup, but Wise didn't think a man like the doctor would know what to do. He'd think his chances of fleeing the country were ruined after he had told Monroe about what he had been up to. Wise didn't think the man would have gone far. He marched through the gate and up the short path to the door and hammered with his fist. "Levison? It's the police," he lied.

He waited less than five seconds before he repeated the knocks and shouts. "Open up, I need to speak to you urgently," he added.

Wise kicked the door in and marched to the stairs. He would have bet his pension that the bastard was still in the house.

He climbed the stairs and found the hatch to the attic. A long pole with a hook on it was tucked into the side of the airing cupboard on the landing.

Wise used the pole to open the hatch and pull the aluminium ladder down. He climbed the steps and poked his head through the open hatch.

"Don't fuck about. I know you're here," he shouted.

He waited a moment and then heard a shuffling in a far corner to his left.

"What do you want?" The accent was clipped, and it reminded Wise of the BBC reporters from half a century ago.

"I'm with the police. I need to speak with you now," Wise repeated.

Levison moved towards the hatch, shuffling on hands and knees in the low roof area. Wise felt the rage again. This man was responsible for the shit that had destroyed him again. As Levison neared the hatch, Wise grabbed his shirt collar and pulled him towards him. The man yelled as Wise stepped down the rungs, dragging Levison headfirst out of the hatch. As his upper body came through the opening, Wise jumped down the last few steps and yanked Levison after him. Levison fell on his shoulders onto the landing floor.

"You and I need to talk," Wise seethed.

"W-ho the h-ell are you?" Levison blustered.

"I'm not someone you want to mess around with. Now, get up off your arse and let's sit down somewhere comfortably, because you have a story to tell me and you'd better make sure it's the truth, the whole truth and nothing but the fucking truth."

Levison rolled over onto his knees to rise when Wise stepped close and grabbed him by the hair.

"What the...?"

"I told you, I want to know everything, and I mean it. There is only going to be one good outcome for you and that is with you living to see another day if you are straight with me. I warn you, I've lost too much today to care what happens to me, understand?

Levison nodded his head but grunted with pain as Wise tightened his grip on his hair.

"Right. Where's the whiskey? I need a whiskey."

Wise let Levison stand and followed him down the stairs and into the living room. Levison took a crystal decanter from a cabinet and two matching crystal glasses. He seemed resigned to his fate. His hands shook as he took a bottle of spirit from a cabinet. The fear in his eyes had gone and Wise knew the man was not going to bluff him. "This is my best. It's fifty years old from the Ilse of Islay."

"Prefer Irish myself but beggars can't be choosers, eh?"

Levison handed Wise the glass. He had poured a generous slosh of the amber liquid. He stared at Wise's face. "You know we can do something with that," he said.

Wise shrugged. "My face? I don't think so. I'm sick of operations."

"No, gene therapy. We can do things now that were just science fiction twenty years ago. It's amazing how the science has advanced, you know?"

"So it seems. Does that extend to bringing dead psychopaths back to life?"

"It wasn't my idea…"

"I don't care, you're just as guilty."

Levison took a long shot of his drink and turned to face the fireplace, seemingly not wanting to look at Wise. "Do you remember the fuss when Dolly the sheep was cloned many years ago?"

"I remember."

"There was an outcry of concern about the moral ethics of carrying out such an experiment. The sheep was created from the genes of another and, in lay-man terms, was the replica of the donor. Of course it was not the same sheep. It was just genetically the same. Just like twins. You can't begin to imagine how excited we were at the lab. We had been commissioned by a department within the government to help the university of London to investigate the psychology of the criminal mind. The work had been started in the early sixties in the US. A Jewish children's adoption agency had been involved in placing twins separated for adoption to families of different social standings. The idea was to monitor the differences and similarities attributable to the nurturing in these diverse environments. The most famous case was the triplets that became famous for finding each other at the age of nineteen. Of course, no one suspected that the separation would cause such devastating effects on the mental health of the children. That was the start. We had to wait many years before the genome research began to offer different possibilities. We had a huge injection of money from a mystery benefactor. It was all systems go. There was already a great deal of research into understanding the outcomes of psychopathy but no real, tangible understanding of the triggers. If we could understand the triggers then we might be able to prevent them or perhaps even reverse them."

"So, your genetic research was into the cause of criminal nutters?"

Levison turned and smiled. "Not exactly how I would put it, but yes. I suppose that's it. In a nutshell."

"~~Okay~~ OK, and?"

"And we began with the existing research, the old stuff, like the triplets, that examined the traits of those twins and triplets separated at birth. There were quite a few to study, more than you would imagine. The Catholics were also a great help. They had caused mayhem in the fifties and sixties, taking the babies of unmarried mothers away and giving them to stable families."

"That was inhuman."

"Maybe so, probably so, but it had happened, and the instances of twins were perfect for the studies into nature or nurture. It was perfect. Two identical twins, separated at birth, sometimes separated by oceans and by social status, would one be more prone to certain psychological trends than another?"

"And?"

"Well, surprisingly, they seemed to exhibit very similar traits, even without knowledge of each other. One twin brought up in a religious household could be expected to be religious but that then didn't account for the twin who might have been brought up in an atheist family, and yet also show similar beliefs as the other. Now how on earth could that be? It had to be genetic."

"And that's when you decided to use gene donors?"

He looked embarrassed for a moment then became excited again. "Can you imagine the importance of this? We set about collecting samples from donors and then secretly implanting these genes to have real babies, babies that were fully mapped for the study. It was amazing. Time and again there were instances of similarities between the twins we had... created."

"Created? You fucked with nature."

"Nonsense. We manipulated nature to our needs but did no more than nature does itself."

"I assume you kept all these twins separate from each other to carry out the research?"

"Of course?"

"And the University was in on this?"

"Of course not. They knew nothing of our… extra work. They would never have condoned it."

"Too ~~royal~~ right they wouldn't. They wouldn't because it's downright inhuman."

"There's no place for sentimentality in this kind of work. Can't you see the importance of what we were doing? You, as an ex-copper should know…"

"You know who I am?"

Levison realised he had said too much but also knew he had to say more. "Of course I know who you are. You are John Wise. There isn't someone else with *your* facial injuries likely to come knocking at my door."

"OK. Then you know that people have been dying horrible deaths and I believe they are connected to these experiments."

The doctor took another long drink, finished his whiskey and poured another for them both. "Yes. I'm afraid it is but you have to believe me when I say it wasn't my call. I was against it…"

"Against what?"

He sighed and necked the whole glass and poured another for himself. "It seemed to make sense to the funders to get to the crux of the question we were researching. They wanted conclusive proof of genetic influence in behaviour of a criminal kind. The only way they could do that was to target living criminals. The research was, at first, inconclusive, but pointed to something that might be responsible, some gene or combination of genes that caused a propensity towards crime. Then it was agreed, at a pay grade way above me, that we should extract samples from well-known criminals... criminals that were convicted, tried and were... let's say... no longer a threat. Criminals with specific M.O. and criminals that would be easy to identify. That's when..."

"That's when you began using samples from historical exhibits."

Levison nodded.

"And someone thought it would be a good idea to try and find the DNA of Jack the Ripper?"

Levison looked shocked. "I had no idea. None of us knew the true identities of those samples. That was the whole point. It had to be blind. It wasn't until the first of the killings that Felicity... the doctor killed in the car park of the lab, began to suspect. She began accessing files that were tagged by the project controllers. I can only assume that they then tested their creation out on her."

"It was a test? They killed an innocent woman for a test?" Wise said, shocked and disgusted by what he had heard.

"Well it was a bit more than that, or at least it became more than that. It seems that the killer also accessed the genetic profiles of all the victims of the Ripper back in the nineteenth century and decided he wasn't satisfied with the what his predecessor had achieved. He wanted to wipe out the DNA of all the victims of the original murders, just because he could."

"You mean to say that he's targeted these women, these victims, because they have the same DNA as the original Ripper's victims?"

Levison nodded. "That's what I'm saying. He's out of control. He has to be stopped. The controllers suspect that I know everything and I'm not safe anymore. I thought it was them at the door when you called."

"Why didn't you just run?"

"Where can I go? I've nowhere to run. I don't have the energy to run."

"Who is this killer, the new Ripper?"

Levison went to a bookcase and opened up a book. It was a so-called expose of the original Ripper.

He held up the book and removed a sheet of paper. "This book? It's way off the mark," he said before he tossed it on the chair. "This is the identity of the killer. His real name is Caine Bartlett. You probably know him as Isaac?"

Wise took the sheet. "Can't be. Isaac has an alibi."

"No. There were two, you see. We created twins for the experiment. Lovely little boys they were, at the beginning. Then things began to change. They were separated and a team of specialist kept tabs on them at all times. Then both of the lads contracted meningitis. One of them failed to recover. We tried everything to save him, but he died. His twin was saved but he lost his foot as a result of the infection. You'd never know it, though. He adapted well, he could run as fast as anyone and didn't even have a limp... unless he wanted to," he smiled, thinking. "He was a devious little boy. If he didn't want to do something he'd limp around and say his foot was causing him problems. Then he'd be running around with the other children without the slightest indication he only had one foot."

"My God. Then if there's two... it makes sense. Isaac didn't have a limp when he was arrested."

"Isaac, the real Isaac, was different. He was a disappointment to the authorities. He showed no sign of psychopathy. He was normal little boy and it seemed to destroy the theory that the genes, would affect the instincts towards crime. He was left with a lovely caring family and his file was closed. Caine's file was closed earlier when he contracted meningitis and supposedly died. That's wrong, of course. He had been earmarked as the child they wanted and, whilst he lost his foot during his illness, that didn't seem to have an impact on him."

"So, Isaac, I mean Caine, has been killing women, the only connection being a genetic one, and the sponsors of the project have been protecting him?"

"They can't let him be caught. They'll make sure he has witnesses to say he was nowhere near any of the killings. They were creating killers they hoped would be of use to them. It's what they do. They've always done it, but they seemed to have a crazy idea that they could make perfect killers, people they could control."

"This is unbelievable."

"But true, none the less."

"OK. If this is true. When did he first kill?"

"That was when he was still a boy. Eight, I think. He had gone with a nanny and some other children to play in the snow. He ran off…"

"What about security?"

"There was security. They always had security. Men who were used to killing, they had to be in case they had to terminate one of the children for some reason."

"My God."

"On this particular occasion, let's call him by his real name, Caine. Caine ran off through woods and the security man was watching. He tried to capture Isaac, but the kid was too clever for him. Slit his throat in the man's car. Caine had worked it out and had hidden in the back and waited for him to return. As I said, Caine is very clever."

"This is doing my head in. Caine is pretending to be his brother, Isaac? Isaac is still alive, obviously, but knew nothing of Caine? So, Caine is one half of a twin. Now he's running around pretending to be both?"

Levison sighed, as if he was fed up with repeating himself but it was complicated and difficult for someone like Wise to grasp. "I only discovered Caine was alive when I accessed the classified files. It was Caine who lost the foot, but he calls himself Isaac when he wants to enjoy his perverse pastime. Some twisted connection to his brother. Understand now?"

Wise didn't look sure but nodded. "Pastime? Are you for real?"

Levison held up his hands. "Sorry, wrong word. But you have no idea how clever Caine is. He truly believes he is the reincarnated Jack the Ripper. He's not, of course, but I no longer know if it's genetic duplication or the fact that the isolation and whatever the hell the controllers have done to him has caused him to be like that. To be honest, I don't care. I just want out."

"Well, Doctor. I think you're in far too deep to just run away."

"What can I do, I've nowhere to run?" Levison looked worried for the first time since Wise had arrived at his house.

"You can help me catch this bastard."

Levison and Wise talked for an hour. Levison described Caine's personality type, a type Wise had met more than once before during his time as a detective. Caine was certainly a sociopath or psychopath; the label didn't matter. He had no empathy, liked to control others and nothing and no one mattered other than himself.

Wise had been through more than most in the last three years and the latest lost had destroyed him. Only his hatred for the killer gave him any kind of focus. It kept him going and he was determined to end the killer's run.

## CHAPTER 40

It would be four or five weeks before Monroe and Sam could be buried. It could even be much longer if the killer wasn't brought to justice soon. After a murder, the pathologist would carry out a post-mortem and the report would be used by the prosecution and defence solicitors. The delay was to allow the defence to call in independent pathologists if necessary and for all evidence relating the cause of death to be explored and exhausted and even agreed before the body was released for burial. Without a suspect, the delay could be much longer. It hurt to think of Sam and his friend not being laid to rest.

The Metropolitan Police had decided to hold a memorial service for Monroe. Thousands of colleagues and members of the public had turned up to pay their respects to a large framed phot of the former senior detective. There was nothing like it organised for Sam. She had no family that he knew of and he felt so sorry for her. There would be no one to mourn her or miss her – except for him.

The church of Our Lady of Lourdes was a typically progressive Catholic design. The hexagonal building with the seven-sided spire was painted white with windows shaped like small crosses all the way up each side.

Lines of uniformed police officers stood outside while over two-hundred other were crammed inside.

Wise stood in the first floor window of an empty flat. The windows had been covered with a white paint to hide the interior from prying eyes and the door to the small two-bed apartment had been easy to break open. The lounge had no furniture, but three wooden packing cases had clearly been used as sets by someone, probably a squatter at some time in the recent past. The bedroom window overlooked the church and Wise rubbed away a small area of the paint to gain a clear view and pulled a box to the window for a seat. It was going to be a long day. He desperately wanted to join the mourners, to show his respect and appreciation for the man who died trying to help him, but Wise was still wanted, and he had to stay free.

It was dark as the last of the mourners walked away from the church.

To pay his respects was a risk he was prepared to take. He owed Monroe that. He knew Catholics lit candles and said prayers for their deceased and the least Wise could do was the same. He'd be in and out before anyone knew he was there. He grabbed a hooded overcoat he had bought earlier to hide his face and set off into the night.

\*\*\*

Out of the dark trees at the rear of the church, a lone figure slowly walked up to the entrance to the presbytery. The figure paused before opening a large wooden door and entered.

\*\*\*

A hooded man watched the figure enter the church. He guessed he would be there, he guessed he would want to gloat. He walked slowly towards the front of the church.

\*\*\*

Another door opened into the church and the man walked past the priest busying himself with a collection of orders of service left by the mourners.

The man entered a confessional and closed the door loudly behind him. The priest looked up and set the pile of papers down on a pew and entered the adjacent booth. He sat and slid a small partition window.

The man next to him inhaled deeply, as if he was sniffing the air.

"Welcome."

"Forgive me Father for I have sinned," the man said.

"Confession is the path to forgiveness."

"You misunderstand me, Father. I'm not here to seek redemption."

"I don't understand."

The man inhaled deeply again.

"Are you OK?" the priest asked.

"I come to deliver a message."

The priest wiped a bead of sweat from his brow. There was a strange tone to the man's voice, a tone that held menace. "What message?"

"We'll get to that in due course. But I have a question for you, Father."

"Are you here to make a confession?"

The man made no replay for a brief second then spoke again. "What do you see when you look in the mirror?"

The priest turned to look at the man, but only sees shadows. He was confused by the question but answered as confidently as he could manage. "When I look in the mirror, I see a man who love God as much as the day I became a priest. I see a man who tries daily to repay the love and trust that has been bestowed upon me."

"Very good, Father. Predictable, but I have no doubt that's what you want others to see but I see something different. I sense you are not what you pretend to be."

The priest froze, a shiver running up his spine. "I don't know what you're talking about."

"I thought the Catholic Church forbade the ordination of women, Father?"

There was no reply.

"Father? Or should I call you mother?"

The priest spluttered, "I don't know what you're talking about."

"Oh, I think you do, Mother. I can smell you."

"You are talking nonsense…"

"Let me tell you what I see when I look in the mirror. I see… I see the end of humanity."

"Why would you say that, why say such a thing? What's causing you this pain? Why are you saying these things about me?"

The world is full of confusion. Men who are women, women who are men, children who don't identify with any sex. Imagine a world where all that ended, where everyone was perfect, even you Father.

The priest took a deep breath. "In God we have the key to solving the word's troubles through love and faith. It's God's will that he gave us the way to seek the solutions that will come through Our Lady, Mary the Mother of God and Jesus…"

"God's will? You think we are equal in God's eyes?"

"Yes, I believe we are equal, at least created equal. We have free will to determine our path..."

The man snapped. "I am not equal You were not created equal, were you Father? Did you tell the Bishop you were born a woman?"

The priest thumped his fist against the partition. "Get out!"

"None of us are equal," the man said. "The human desire for power. Even the Church hordes its wealth at the expense of the sheep that blindly follow. That will end you. For that there is no truth in your God."

The priest took several deep breaths. He had to stay calm. "None of us are perfect," he whispered, "but God is our Creator; you must have faith that His plan will be fulfilled."

The man laughed. "I *do* have faith, faith in the inevitability that man will die. And for the record, Father... we are most definitely not created equally. God had no hand in my creation and if he had a hand in yours, he clearly fucked it up."

The priest felt his chest tighten. He took a small tablet from a pot in his pocket and placed it under his tongue.

\*\*\*

Caine stepped out of the confessional and walked towards the exit. The priest followed at a distance. Confused by the strange words of the man who was walking towards a hooded figure standing in the doorway of the church.

Stopping at the first pew, Caine placed a piece of folded paper on the seat as the hooded spectre walked towards him. Caine kept his eyes on the hood, the face lost in shadows. The man had come for him, it was obvious, and he began to smile.

The dishevelled man in the hooded coat shook with anger as he neared but the man stooped in front of him and raised his arms like Jesus on the cross.

The voice from the hood cracked with emotion as a second World War handgun is pulled from the coat as he pulled the hood from his face and pointed the weapon at Caine. "It's you… it's you, you son of a bitch. You took my baby, my sweet Cindy."

Charlie's distraught features made Caine laugh harder. "I thought it was the charred copper," Caine roared, "but it's just some old man."

Charlie's hands were shaking so much that Caine shook his head in disappointment. He slowly grabbed the gun and steadied the barrel for Charlie to aim it against his forehead.

"Are you insane?" Charlie gasped.

"How did you find me?"

"The funeral of one of the coppers ~~tracking~~helped me track you down. I guessed you'd want to come and see the pain you've caused, you sick fuck."

You want revenge, don't you? Well here's your shot. One shot, straight and true. One shot for sweet little... Cindy, was it? Not that I have any idea who fucking Cindy is or was. I presume she was one of the tarts I dispatched?"

"Don't you dare call Cindy a tart," Charlie spluttered, spittle flying from his lips, his hand began to lose aim and Caine leaned his forehead tight against the barrel. Charlie backed off a step, but his nerves were destroying his plan. He had to put the bastard down. He had to. He saw the priest run for cover just as his finger closed on the trigger. Even at close range he misses the shot. He had the chance to finish it, to end the nightmare this creature had created for him and Martha and he couldn't even do that one thing. Charlie collapsed to the floor in tears. The killer looked momentarily confused and knelt down next to him.

"What are you going to do?" Charlie sobbed.

"You're not on my list, your wife is because she carries the gene that has to end. However, you did try to kill me, and we can't have that, now can we?" he smiled sweetly. Caine ran his hands through Charlie's hair and down his face. Calmly he pulled his scalpel from his coat and cut Charlie's throat.

The priest, hiding behind a wooden pillar behind them screamed, "Who are you?"

"Read the note, Father," Caine said as he stood and walked away down the aisle towards the exit.

The priest hurried to the pew and picked up the note. There were just five terrifying words, 'YOURS TRULY, JACK THE RIPPER.'

***

The gunshot had Wise breaking cover. He ran towards the door of the church and stopped outside. He put his ear against the heavy oak door and listened briefly before he turned the big metal ring and pulled the door towards him.

A dark figure lay in the middle of the aisle, blood seeping across the marble floor. A priest stood over the prone figure, frozen, his face a mask of horror.

Wise stepped inside the church as a figure appeared at his side.

"Too late. I expected you earlier," a voice whispered in his ear.

Wise turned to face the voice, but the figure had gone, seemingly melted into thin air.

"That's him," the priest shouted.

Wise looked around him, where had he gone? How had he just disappeared?

"Out, he's gone out through the door," the priest shouted again, as if reading Wise's mind.

Wise ran out through the door but there was no sign of Caine. He had missed his chance. The man had gone. Then he saw movement, a dark figure heading towards the entrance to the underground station.

## CHAPTER 41

The thunderous noise of a train pulling away from the platform shook the tunnel as Wise reached the bottom of the escalator. The station was empty, but he caught sight of a man ducking out of sight and onto the platform. The train had left so Wise had him. There was nowhere Caine could go other than into the track tunnel. Wise slowed as he reached the platform, senses on high alert. Caine was nowhere in sight. He had gone left, so Wise knew he had to be on the track following the direction of the train.

He lit a cigarette to calm his nerves and walked on until he saw a light up ahead. He pulled a torch from his coat, dropped down onto the tracks and walked on towards the light.

Wise kept clear of the live rail and moved quickly. The last thing he wanted was to get caught by a train. At least he knew he'd hear it coming.

He had walked nearly thirty metres when the rancid smell of rotting flesh brought him to a halt. He gagged and covered his nose with his left hand.

A rusty metal door in the old brick wall to his left was ajar. Wise pushed through the gap and entered a very dark room. Using the torch, he scanned the space, the smell was almost too much for him.

The beam of light from the torch falls across the disembowelled body of a young woman.

Wise stumbled out of the room, fells to his knees and threw up.

He heard something; a noise somewhere close.

A light in the room behind him switched on and startled him, flooding a section of the railway line. Turning off the torch he entered once more. Stepped over the remains of the woman and headed towards a door at the far end. The light switch was on the wall next to the open door. Wise slipped on body fluids and lost his balance. As he rights himself the light goes off, plunging him into total darkness. "Shit, shit, shit," he whispered to himself. He fumbled the torch but the light switches on again but there was no one near the light switch.

He set off slowly, cautiously, more alert than he had ever been. He had already taken a tumble and he couldn't afford to make another mistake. He had to end Caine's reign of terror her and now. He entered the passageway through the open door and climbed a series of concrete steps before meeting a large steel door with newly oiled hinges. He took a deep breath then gripped the handle and pulled the door open. He leapt through the door to be greeted by hordes of startled people on a busy platform of another underground station.

Embarrassed, Wise smiled at the people near to him and disappeared back into the stairwell. The poor soul disembowelled in the room below had to be recovered for her family to get closure. He had no idea how long she had been down there but, judging by the rate of decay and the feeding of rats Wise guessed it had been at least a week.

He pulled a handkerchief from his pocket and tied is around his head and over his nose and mouth. It did little to offset the stench, but it still somehow seemed necessary.

Wise carefully lifted a gnawed leather coat that was lying near the body to check for identification and jumped when a mobile phone to ring. It was somewhere inside a pocket of the coat. Wise fumbled through the pockets and found a cheap brand phone. It lacked the capabilities of other more expensive models but clearly could pick up a signal below ground. He checked the caller I.D., hoping it might be a family member checking on the victim's whereabouts, but the screen text read 'Caller Withheld.'

He pressed the green accept button and held the phone to his ear.

"Who is this?"

"Hello, John."

"Who is this?" Wise had already knew the answer.

"You should know the answer to that. After all, you are the one looking for me."

"How the hell did you know I'd find the phone and answer?"

"There are eyes everywhere these days, John. You, being and ex-copper should know that better than most."

Wise peered around the room looking for a C.C.T.V. camera. There it was, a small unit the size of a box of matches, fixed to a corner at ceiling height. He stood and walked towards the camera. He stared straight into the lens. "I swear to Christ I'm going to kill you."

"John, please... we both know you're in no fit shape to carry out such a threat. Besides, I feel your hatred of me is misplaced. We may have more in common than you realise."

Wise laughed but there was no humour in the sound. "What could you possibly think we have in common?"

"We both live on the edge. We love the thrill of the chase, playing the game."

"You think this is a game?"

"A game of life, a game of death. A game we both play until one of us is no longer exits, then it's game over."

"I understand just fine, I understand that you're living in a world of your own. You are not firing on all four cylinders. But guess what? This sick game of yours, you fucker, is a game you'll lose."

"That's the spirit, John. Your friends would be proud, if they were alive," he laughed. "You know, the Superintendent and, what was her name… Samantha? Pretty girl. Just like your sister."

"My sister?" Wise felt a growing sense of dread.

"You know she's been discharged from hospital? The cops charged her with stealing the car, but she seemed to be OK when she got home to the cinema."

The bastard knew where she lived, and Wise knew he had to get to her before Caine. The madman was telling him where he was and what he would do next, the sick bastard. "You've done enough. She doesn't have anything to do with this. If you're targeting the genes, then my sister doesn't fit your profile." Wise was trying anything and everything to stop Caine, but he knew the man just enjoyed killing. The excuse of ending the genes was just that.

"But that's just it, John. Don't you understand? Do you think this is just chance, serendipity? You think we live our lives in isolation with no great universal plan? The universe works in strange and wonderful ways. Our paths crossed because we had no say in the matter. You have been brought to me because you too, you and your sister are part of the game, you carry the genes of one of the original victims. Seems you are ordained to be a victim."

Wise didn't know what to say. There was no connection between him and any of the original Ripper victims, at least none that he knew of. Caine was just nuts. "Bollocks," he said as he began to run towards the stairwell and onto the platform. The signal broke and he stuffed the phone into his pocket.

He sprinted onto the street and headed to the taxi rank. The phone rang in his pocket. "You won't make it in time, I'm afraid."

Wise dialled Martine's number at the theatre. He had to warn her.

A taxi pulled up in the rank and Wise opened the back door. "Hey, you have to take the front car," the driver protested.

A queue of a dozen people was already in the line and Wise couldn't wait. He slammed the door and ran around to the driver's door. He yanked it open and pulled the driver out and bundled him onto the road.

"What the fu...?" the driver shouted.

Wise could see the others in the queue were looking at him in shock and a driver of a cab ahead had seen him and was getting out of his cab to help his fallen colleague.

Jumping behind the wheel, Wise put the cab in gear and pulled out of the line and accelerated past the advancing cabbie who was forced to dive into the gap between two other cabs.

***

The pain in Martine's head had eased, the medication had done its magic, but she felt nauseous. She felt like shit, dirty and confused. She had hated her brother for too long, blaming him for a deadly situation that had ended her husband's life, but she had always really known he wasn't to blame. She had just needed someone to hang the death on, someone who's actions had directly turned the events that day and that someone was John. She climbed the stairs slowly and entered the bathroom. She ran the hot water and poured some fancy brand bubbles directly into the steaming stream. A bath would revive her, freshen her body and hopefully clear her head. The sound of the running water drowned out the ring tone of her house phone in the living room next door.

Martine knew the people responsible for her husband's death were the thugs that triggered the events that followed. Had they not tried to rob the bank then John wouldn't have been called.

Slipping off her pyjamas, she folded them neatly and piled them on the top of the laundry basket next to the shower cubicle. She set the D.A.B. radio to Radio Two and added cold water to the bath and stepped into the foaming water.

The house phone rang again but the sound was no match for Freddie Mercury as he sang, 'who wants to live forever?' Martine sang along. She loved Queen.

\*\*\*

The stolen cab sped down the road, screaming round corners as Wise banged on the horn to clear the way.

"Move it, get out the way," he shouted through the open window.

\*\*\*

Martine pulled the plug and dried herself as the water drained from the tub. She donned a clean pair of pyjamas and her robe and sang along to an Elvis song. She stepped out into the hallway and stopped as the buzzer to the flat began to sound. She frowned and then smiled, perhaps John had got away? She opened the flat door and descended the stairs to the private entrance at the side of the cinema. She could see the figure of a man through the frosted glass front door. It certainly looked the same size and shape as her brother.

"Thought they'd locked you up?" she said as she opened the door. For a brief moment she stood surprised to see a strange man, then the confusion turns to fear as the man began to grin.

***

Shouting at passing traffic was useless but somehow seemed essential to him, the sounds of the traffic probably blotted out anything he was shouting, and he couldn't hear anything that was being shouted back at him. Wise was shaking with fear and equal amounts of anger.

***

Martine was too slow, Caine pushed her back onto the stairs and slammed the door behind him before grabbing Martine's throat. She tried to scream but couldn't make a sound.

Caine held her against the, right hand at her throat, left hand on her shoulder and his right knee pressed into her stomach and snarled at her. "I can make this easy or very, very hard," he said. "Shall we have a cup of tea and a chocolate biscuit? I love chocolate biscuits. Do you have any?" Now he smiled.

She tried to nod; her eyes wide in terror.

He eased the pressure on her throat. "One more scream or sound that is higher than a whisper and I'll have to silence you permanently, understand?"

Now she could nod properly. "Yes," she gasped.

He grabbed he by her hair and dragged Martine up the stairs and into the lounge. He stopped and looked around the room. "Nice place." He looked at the collection of movie posters on the walls and threw her to the floor. "One Million Years BC," he said as he pointed at a poster featuring Raquel Welsh dressed in animal skins that barely covered her modesty. "Loved that film. The dinosaurs were stop motion; did you know that?"

Martine grunted, "Yes."

"Jurassic Park was light years ahead in terms of animation, but I still love that old film."

He moved along the line of posters, all mounted with white surrounds and framed in black wood. "Frankenstein? Boris Karloff. My hero. We have a lot in common, you know?" He looked at Martine as she slowly slithered away from him. "I'd stop there, if I were you. You have nowhere to run." His voice was low and calm. He pulled the scalpel from his pocket and placed the it on the coffee table and then took a Magnum_.45 from his coat pocket and checked the cylinder. He smiled again. "Just in case your brother wants to try something," he explained and placed the gun alongside the blade. "He should be hear soon," he said.

***

The cab screeched to a halt at the front of the cinema. The place had remained closed since Martine had left with him days earlier. A poster she had written and affixed to the Art Nouveau doors announcing the temporary suspension of business. Wise abandoned the cab with the engine still running and raced around to the side entrance to the flat.

***

"The Blob, Steve McQueen's first break," Caine said as he continued checking out the posters.

"Wouldn't take you for a film buff," Martine croaked, her throat still sore.

"We make sweeping assumptions that are mostly wrong. Who'd have doubted the words of the doctor when they said my twin brother had died from the meningitis?"

"Look, take the posters, they're worth a small fortune, all originals from when my father and grandfather had the cinema."

Caine ignored her. "Strange how fate brings us together, isn't it? Did you know, for example, that your great grandmother's sister was the victim of the original Jack the Ripper?"

Martine sat up. "No. That can't be. Someone would have told my granddad."

He shook his head. "Nah, probably ashamed that she was a common prostitute."

Martine felt angry. "She was a woman, entitled to her life. I don't care of she was a relative, she didn't deserve to die like she did at the hands of a madman."

He spun on his heels to stare at her. "Madman? You think the Ripper was mad?"

"He was a psychopath."

He leaned towards her, his face close to hers. "Labels. Labels don't tell the story. He wasn't mad, he was a genius."

Now Martine laughed. "I get it, you think you're fucking Jack the Ripper."

He shook his head and glared at her, his eyes blazing with anger. "I don't think I'm the Ripper. I AM the Ripper. I'm the ultimate example of science perfecting the human line for the betterment of the planet. I'm one of the first to prove that our destiny lies in our own hands."

"You're the ultimate example of a fucked-up nutter."

Caine raised his hand to strike her across the face when the door to the flat burst open and Wise stood in the doorway, quickly scanning the scene before him. Caine stood over his sister and he saw the gun and the blade on the table next to Caine.

"You were quick," Caine said as he straightened and grabbed both the scalpel and the gun.

Wise raised his hands in the air, it was a pointless exercise, but it seemed to be the thing to do, that's what they did in films.

"Look at you," Caine laughed. "You didn't have much luck last time you walked in on my family."

Confused, Wise shook his head. "What the fuck are you talking about?"

"Your face. Your brother-in-law. Tragic. Such a shame but you really pissed me off," Caine began to raise his voice. "You should have stayed out of the bank. No one had to get hurt. You killed my friends," he took a deep breath and lowered voice, "or... shall we say... my cousins?"

"Your cousins? They were just bank robbers, stupid idiots. You have a twin, but you don't have any other family. Isaac isn't really family either, is he? He's just a fucking clone, like a sheep."

"I see you've done your homework."

"I'm a copper."

"No. You were a copper. Now you're just an ugly fuck with a face like a piece of liver."

Wise felt the anger rise inside, not from the insults, he'd grown used to callous comments since his injury, throw away remarks that were intended to hurt. He was beginning to feel the rage that he had threatened to overwhelm him when this man had killed Sam. Sam, the woman who had offered a chance for him, a chance for a life as normal as he could ever hope for.

Caine didn't pick up on the change that was taking over Wise. "My brother recovered from the meningitis. He was too soft for them. They had other plans for me, pretended that I'd died because they had seen something special in me. They had other plans for us all, they needed to clear the decks, to make people think that he and the others had died. There was twenty or so of us in all. Most were killed as kids, some grew up and began to show their true breeding. The robbers were from the project, a test, given free rein and they proved they were 'a chip off the old block' so to speak," he laughed. "Come in and close the door," he continued, "You're letting the heat out. Just think about your sister's heating bill," he sniggered, "but then, I don't suppose she'll be around to pay it."

Wise stepping into the room and closed the door behind him. Caine waved him towards the settee. He had to stall the madman, distract him long enough to try something. He had no idea what he could do but he knew he had to do something. Caine indicated for Martine to join her brother.

Martine crawled past Caine and sat alongside Wise.

"This bollocks about you being the Ripper…"

"Bollocks?" Caine interrupted. "It's not bollocks. I didn't choose to be like this," he said. "None of us chose to be like this. We were fucking experiments. Surrogate mothers from broken families desperate for cash. Genetic engineering paid for by billionaires who dreamt of changing the world, of creating the traits they wanted to do their bidding," his voice rose again. "Do you know how that must feel, to be nothing more than a fucking experiment?"

"I know what it's like to be different."

"Of course you do. Look at you. I can barely stomach you."

"At least I've still got my humanity."

Caine laughed again. "Humanity? We're all nothing but little piggies, animals in a pen with no control of our destiny. You have no idea who's been bank rolling this project."

"So tell me," Wise said.

"If I told you, you ~~you~~ wouldn't believe me."

"Try me."

Caine paused for a moment, considering whether to reveal his secret but then pointed the gun at Wise. "On your feet, the two of you. We're going to watch a film. What have we got?"

"Frozen 2 or Angel has Fallen," Martine said.

"As much as I love animation, I think a bit of Gerard Butler is more to my taste."

They walked ahead of Caine and took the door leading to the staircase that descended into the foyer of the cinema. Martine flicked a light switch and stepped aside for her brother and the gun-toting Caine to join her.

"I love the smell of popcorn," Caine said as he breathed deeply. "You go and run the film while your brother and I go and get some seats. Fancy some popcorn or a soft drink?" he asked Wise.

"I'd rather smash you in the face and kick your fucking head into next week," he said calmly.

Caine shrugged. "Suit yourself."

Martine opened the door to the projector room.

"No tricks, no calling for help. Remember I have a gun pointing at lizard man here," he warned her.

She looked at her brother and he winked. He mouthed 'I love you,' and she smiled before climbing another staircase up to the projector room.

Caine kept the gun pointing at Wise's head as they entered the theatre and walked down the aisle.

"Keep going," he said.

Wise walked until they reached the front row of seats.

"This will do," he pointed towards the seats in the middle of the line. "You sit in front and I'll sit behind you, just in case you get some stupid idea.

"You are fucking crazy, you know that?"

"Just sit and shut the fuck up," Caine said. "Remember to ensure your phone is switched off and don't disturb others by talking over the film."

The film began and the theatre was filled with dancing light and colours.

Wise walked slowly along the front row and Caine shuffled between the seats of the row behind. He had made a mistake. Wise saw his chance as Caine caught his leg against a chair and was momentarily distracted. Wise dived across the back of the seats and hit Caine as he pulled the trigger. The round hit Wise in his left thigh and he cried out in pain as he felt it pass through the flesh and out through the other side. Wise drove his head into Caine's nose and felt it break. He could see the blood on the man's face, but

Caine was grinning as he brought the gun up towards Wise. Wise grabbed the gun hand and pushed it away and then down hard on to the back of the chair. Caine grunted as the gun fell from his hand and bounced off the seat. The weapon hit the floor and skittered across the floor towards the screen. Wise punched Caine in the face but the man was still grinning. Then Wise saw why. Caine had the scalpel in his other hand and he thrust it into Wise's cheek. The scar tissue split and Wise cried out again. Caine had missed his eye but the blade had past through the cheek into his mouth. Wise pulled away and fell back over the chair, the blade slicing through his mouth as he fell.

Wise could see the gun just feet away and scrambled towards it as Caine dived over the row of seats and land on top of him. Wise felt the blade pierce his shoulder and then his back. He grasped the gun and swung it around as Caine kept stabbing him with the scalpel. Caine saw the gun and dropped the blade to grab the gun. They rolled on the floor and Caine pulled the weakened Wise over on top of him. Now Wise was lying on Caine facing up towards the screen.

Then the blade was back at his throat. Caine had it in his hand again. Wise waited for the blade to end his life. He could feel his strength draining from him along with his blood. Caine would be doing him a favour but Martine would still be at his mercy.

"Get on your feet," Caine hissed in his ear.

Both men struggled to their feet and Caine stayed behind Wise, knife poised at his throat. The gun was still in Wise's hand, but he knew he would never have the time to get a shot off before Caine cut his throat.

The two men stood in front of the ceiling to floor screen, their shadows cast against the moving image behind them.

Wise looked towards the projector room. The light blinded him, but he thought he saw the outline of his sister's head alongside the lens. He had always loved Martine and it had crushed him when she had distances herself from him. Now he knew they were ~~okay~~ OK. She would not hate him any longer. He turned the gun in to his own chest. He would see to it that Caine's reign of terror ended here and now. He felt his legs begin to give under him. He took a deep breath and smiled as he pulled the trigger.

***

Martine had seen her brother look towards her. He was smiling as he shot himself. The sound of the gun was deafening, even above the soundtrack of the movie. Martine saw her brother collapse to the floor and Caine remained standing, shocked.

She ran for the door and clambered down the steep stairs to the foyer. She pulled open the door to the theatre and ran towards her brother. She didn't care about Caine. But Caine turned towards her, the grin was fading as he too began to collapse to his knees. Martine stopped short of the mad man and saw the bloom of red appear on his chest. Caine fell onto his side. Wise had sacrificed himself to kill the Ripper.

Martine stepped over Caine and grabbed the gun. Her brother's eyes were open. She knelt next to him and held his head in her hands.

"John, can you hear me?"

"Of course I can hear you. I'm shot not deaf."

She forced a smile but knew her brother was slipping away.

"I'm sorry, John, so sorry about..."

He lifted his hand slightly and rolled his head. "No need. I'm sorry I won't be around to help you with the cinema. I always loved this place... and... I always loved you..."

His eyes closed and Martine knew he had gone.

The tears blurred her eyes as she heard a movement behind her. She spun to see Caine sitting up and grinning at her. Martine lifted the gun and pointed it at his head. "I'm going to enjoy cleaning your bloody genes off my fucking floor," she said as she pulled the trigger.

Caine's head exploded as the .45 round entered his face. The smile was fixed as he fell back onto the floor.

## CHAPTER 42

The bodies of Wise and Caine were carried out of the cinema by men in white coveralls.

The police had arrived within five minutes of her call and had secured the cinema for the inevitable investigation.

Detective Inspector Rickett had introduced himself to Martine as she sat at in the foyer. A policewoman stood alongside her as Rickett explained that her brother was no longer a suspect for the death of the old woman. "Bit late now," she said. "I thought you coppers looked after each other?"

Rickett was clearly embarrassed.

Martine watched the men in white as they walked towards the exit. She stood when she saw a logo on the back of the coveralls - 'Innovations Laboratories.'

She walked up to a man with them who was clearly in charge of the others. "Where are you taking them?"

The man turned towards her. "We've been appointed to handle the removal. I'm sorry for your loss."

Martine drew back her fist and hit him square in the jaw.

## Future's Past by David j Henson

***

<u>A Month Later...</u>

A ~~young attractive~~ <u>strikingly attractive</u> woman was writing into a notebook. Her red hair was pulled back into bunches on the side of her head and a thin string of pearls around her neck was almost the same colour as her skin. She sat in a small, featureless white room. opposite the suited man from the cinema. His jaw was red, and he absentmindedly rubbed it with his hand as he watched her.

The woman was writing her name over and over, line after line. She placed the pen on the table and picked up a pencil. Her <u>blank</u> expression changed briefly – a hint of a smile – before she stabbed the pencil down into the man's hand.

***

<u>Airfield in Kent – the Next Day.</u>

The large propellers of a transport plane boomed and began to spin. Thick black smoke bellowed from the engine exhausts as the load bay door is closed.

Two large crates, each big enough to contain a body are marked as 'Biohazard' and are the only cargo.

The attractive red head with her hair in bunches sat in a load bay seat. Her arms were held securely by handcuffs as she stared at the crates.

Doctor Levison and Big Mike sat well away from the woman. They both knew what she was capable of.

The pilot tapped the GPS and input the identity code for the private airfield in New Mexico and ran through the final checks with the co-pilot.

As the props gained speed the roar of the engines echoed across the disserted field.

## References:

https://www.livescience.com/47288-twin-study-importance-of-genetics.html

Printed in Great Britain
by Amazon